1

KAT

Blood splatters across my face, and I scream, turning my head away as I drop to my hands and knees again.

I smell vomit, bullets, and blood, that sweet scent of marshmallow pancakes long gone now.

Another shot is fired, and I fall flat, my hand sliding in something wet and slippery. I scream, and when my scream ends and the sound of bullets is an echo, I roll onto my back, my head heavy, vision fading as I realize something. The thing that terrifies me more than anything else.

Josh has stopped screaming.

The thought of why that could be twists my stomach, and I open my mouth to scream, but the sound that comes isn't human. It's ugly and hoarse and like that of a wounded animal. A dying one.

"Kat?"

I blink, seeing movement above me. Someone's hands are on me, turning me. Instinct takes hold, and I fight. I fight him, but he's too strong. He takes hold of my wrists and lays my arms at my sides.

He mutters a curse. Another shadow passes over me and I'm lifted off the ground. My head hangs, my arms and legs useless as I'm carried through the living room. Two bodies lie on the floor, but I can't make out who they are.

"Lev."

Blood specks every surface, walls and furniture alike, and just before the icy air hits me, I see those muddy boots. Andrei's dirty boots.

I try to lift my head, my arms. Was I shot?

"Just try to relax, Kat."

I'm pushed into the back seat of an SUV. My head lolls against the leather back, and it takes all I have to keep my eyes open. The door closes, and I feel myself slide down toward the opposite corner.

A moment later, that door is opened. I blink, opening my mouth to scream, but it's Lev. It's Lev, and I want to cry.

"Shh. It's okay. You're going to be okay." He's wiping my face with a wet towel. "I need to get Josh. He's going to be scared, Kat. Do you understand?"

"Josh."

"We don't have any time. I need you to help me now, okay? I need you to help Josh."

I nod.

"Good. We need to clean you up at least a little. Can you do that for me while I get Josh?"

I nod again, unable to speak. I take the towel and look down at my bloody hands. I wipe them, but it's impossible to get it all off, and I don't need to see my face to know what it looks like.

Lev is gone, the door closed, but a moment later, he's back, and Josh is clutching Wally and clinging to him as he sobs in his arms. He stops crying when he raises his head and sees me, but then his face contorts, and my heart breaks as a look of horror distorts his features.

His lip trembles as Lev puts him into the seat beside me, and I don't think he can speak. I think he's in shock.

"It's okay, baby," I say, wanting to comfort him, but my voice sounding strange.

Lev looks at us, his face one of utter regret. "I have to get Pasha."

He closes the door before I can ask if he's okay.

I tuck Josh into my side, and he curls into me, hugging Wally under his arm, thumb in his mouth, his other hand around a lock of my hair and I think he's going to get blood on him. I think I shouldn't let him touch me.

Shit.

"We're okay, baby." I try for a soothing voice as I pet his head and he closes his eyes. "We're okay."

The passenger side door opens, and Lev helps Pasha in. I can see in the way he walks that he's hurt, but he manages to turn the visor down and look back at us in the mirror.

"Is Josh hurt?" he asks.

I shake my head.

"I shouldn't...have left." I see the effort it takes him to speak.

"We're okay." We're not, though. Not even close.

Lev climbs into the driver's seat and backs the SUV out of the driveway. As soon as we're on the road, he's making a call. It's a video call, which surprises me.

A man's face comes on the screen, and I don't know how Lev can sound so together, so calm as he speaks. I don't think the man can see us, but I listen, and I think Lev is explaining what happened.

Pasha takes the phone from his hand a moment later, and I think he's attempting a joke, but I can hear that he's in pain.

Andrei must have shot him.

Andrei. What happened to Andrei?

Lev disconnects the call and makes an illegal U-turn at the next traffic light. He glances back at Josh and me, his forehead lined with worry.

"He's asleep?" he asks, eyes half on the road, half on me in the rearview mirror.

I nod.

"You're hurt."

"I'll be okay."

"I'm sorry, Kat. I shouldn't have left you."

"What happened to Andrei?"

"I emptied my gun into him," he says through gritted teeth.

"He's your cousin?" I remember him from the first night at the club, but I didn't know they were cousins. And this thing between them, it goes beyond that. It's very personal.

"He *was* Vasily's son. He murdered my mother. On my uncle's order." Lev's knuckles grow white on the steering wheel as he merges onto the highway north. I remember the conversation he had with Andrei. I knew he was buying time, but they spoke in Russian, so I couldn't understand what he was saying. It must have been this. Did he just find out?

"Andrei is Vasily's son?" I ask, just registering the information.

Lev nods.

Which makes Andrei a blood relation. Vasily is Lev's uncle, and from what I understand, his boss. He's also the man Nina's father stole that flash drive from; the contents of which I've seen.

A new panic takes hold of me.

We're not safe. We're nowhere near safe. And that stolen flash drive that started all of this? It's nothing compared to this. Compared to Lev killing Vasily's son.

"What happens now?"

Lev takes a deep breath in, eyes fixed on the road.

"We're going to Boston. Pasha needs a doctor. One we can trust. Then...we'll see."

2
LEV

"Levka." Alexei opens the door to greet us, gesturing us inside with a solemn expression. This isn't exactly the reunion either of us were expecting, but it is what it is.

"Allow me to help." He takes some of the burden off my shoulders as he slips his arm around Pasha's right side, helping him through the entrance. "Dr. Shtein is upstairs."

I glance back at Kat, who is still in a daze but trying to hold it together for Josh as she cradles him against her chest. More than anything, I want to take them both into my arms and make them forget everything that happened today. But any comfort I might be able to provide will have to wait. The priority right now is ensuring their safety, and there isn't much time.

Magda, the housekeeper, enters the room, with Alexei's wife, Talia, not far behind, and they quickly take it upon themselves to assist in any way they can.

"You've been through quite the ordeal, I'm told," Magda says. "Let me show you to the bathroom where you can clean up, and then I'll fix you something warm to drink. Maybe a snack for the little one?"

Kat looks at me, her eyes clouded and her emotions too raw to make any decisions right now. She's functioning on autopilot, and I can't blame her for that. Sometimes, I forget that most people haven't witnessed the same level of violence as I have in my life. That isn't what I want for Kat. I want her to stay human for as long as possible.

"It's okay." I reach out with my free hand to graze her face. "Magda will take good care of you. Josh is probably hungry. Let him have a snack, and if you want to see me, I'll be upstairs, okay?"

Her eyes are glassy as she nods. Though I don't doubt she's still uncertain, she's aware that right now we have to focus on getting Pasha upstairs.

"It's okay, sweetheart," I assure her as I continue toward the stairs. "One step at a time, alright? For Josh."

Again, she nods, and Magda leads her away with Talia beside them. I hope Kat will feel comfortable with them, but regardless, we won't be staying here for very long.

Alexei and I manage to drag Pasha upstairs to one of the spare bedrooms where Dr. Shtein is waiting. I don't know much about her, other than she often assists with Vory situations such as these. Already, she has Alexei's room set up with medical supplies, and she seems to be familiar with the place as she helps us navigate Pasha to the bed.

"He has two gunshot wounds," I tell her as she begins her physical examination. "One in the thigh and one in the shoulder."

Pasha is covered in blood, but I don't know how much is his and how much is Andrei's. Right now, he looks weak, but he's still conscious, so I figure that has to count for something.

"I will start my work," Dr. Shtein answers briskly. "It is best if you go for now."

Alexei nods, but before we leave the room, I take a moment to thank Pasha for his help. I can't be certain if he hears any of my softly spoken words until he offers me a weak smile.

"I'll be fine," he rasps. "Take care of your family."

I squeeze his hand in mine and then take my leave, following Alexei down the hall to his office. As much as I'd like to stay and wait out the news of Pasha's prognosis, it's a luxury we don't have.

There is no telling how long we have before

Vasily discovers Andrei is dead, but I intend to be out of here before nightfall. Alexei will be one of his first contacts, given that he is my cousin. And while I trust Alexei to honor our safety, he can't do that if we are hiding out in his house. For now, the best thing he can do is extend some of his resources.

"I have one of my men preparing a car for you," Alexei says, taking a seat at his desk so he can face me. "I have provided food, some weapons, and secure phones for you."

"Thank you, Lyoshenka." My voice feels fragile as I study him. This man is my blood, but I have never done anything to warrant such loyalty. I know it is simply because he understands better than anyone the complications of being connected to the Vory while trying to protect your family.

"There is a brownstone set up in Boston," he continues. "It belongs to a friend, but it is available for your family if you wish."

I consider his offer, but as much as I trust Alexei, I don't want to place my family's well-being in anyone else's hands, friend or not.

"I think it will be best for us to stay in some short-term accommodations for now," I answer. "But I appreciate the offer."

He nods as if to say he understands. "Very well. Now I believe we must get to the business of what your plans are."

A caustic laugh chokes the answer from my lips. "Andrei is dead. Vasily will not accept this. He won't let this slight go unpunished."

"So you could run." Alexei shrugs. "But you are not a man to run."

"No," I admit. "I'm not."

Alexei unfolds his hands and reaches down into one of the drawers of his desk, retrieving a brown paper folder. "I've been going through the names on the drive, and I found something this morning. I think you may want to take this into consideration while you are making those plans."

"What is it?" I ask.

He slides the folder across the desk, and when I open it, I find the typical background reports, birth certificate, and health records. Things that Alexei can easily access, given his computer skills. But it is the name on the records that has captured my attention.

"Kieran March?" I murmur, recognizing the similarity to the last name Kat had been using in Colorado. She had called herself Katie March, which is no coincidence. But it isn't until I find a photograph of the woman in the file that it all begins to make sense. She has the same light green eyes. The same red hair. Too many similarities to ignore.

"Kat is…"

"Her daughter," Alexei confirms. "Do you

remember I told you her mother died in the car accident? This is her. For some reason, her name seems to be coded, at least partially. Her real name was Ciara March, and the accident that killed her is no longer looking like a tragic twist of fate, but something intentional."

His words sink into my gut like a stone as I flip through the records of Kat's mother. It doesn't make any sense. Why would her name be on that flash drive? And why would Vasily want her dead?

"I don't understand the connection." I study the information in front of me. "How could Vasily possibly know Kat's mother?"

"Perhaps you need to ask Katerina."

"She isn't aware." I shake my head. "You said yourself she was only three when her mother died. But she was in the car that day. Do you think Vasily knows that Kat is her daughter?"

Alexei shrugs. "I doubt it. She's been using a different name for many years. It's unlikely he's made the connection yet, but it's only a matter of time until he does. If her mother's name was on that list, he wanted her dead for a reason. Now we just have to figure out what that reason was."

"Do you have any leads?" I ask.

"I believe I may have found a fellow Vor connection," he informs me. "You may remember him from your younger years. Does Maxim Sobol sound familiar?"

"Maxim?" I echo. "The guy who used to run jobs for Vasily? He's dead. He's been dead for years. His name is on that list."

"But I think, perhaps, he is not so dead after all." A smile curves Alexei's lips. "I think that's just what he wants Vasily to believe."

It seems like a stretch to bank on a former associate, but I do remember Maxim. He actually helped train me. I ran some of my first jobs with him, and I respected him. But Vasily told me that he killed him. He said Maxim had betrayed him, and I never questioned it further. Now, I wonder what he might have been hiding all these years if he really is alive.

"He worked with Vasily for many years," I note.

"Exactly." Alexei smiles. "One can only imagine the things he might know. Just give me a few more days. Let me see what I can do to draw him out."

I nod, accepting that this will take time. But right now, time isn't on our side. And I can't even begin to imagine how this news will go over with Kat when she finds out. It's unlikely she is even aware of it yet, but at some point, it will need to come out.

"There is something else." I close the folder and tuck it into my jacket for the time being. "I haven't had the chance to tell you, but I found my mother's trinket box in Andrei's garage. When I confronted him, he claimed he was the one who killed her."

"Do you believe him?" Alexei's brows pinch together in uncertainty.

"I do," I confess. "But he claims my mother was going to turn on Vasily. That she was giving information to a neighbor."

"Perhaps the neighbor on the list?" Alexei ventures.

"That was my first thought."

"I will see if I can make a connection."

"Thank you." I reach out to shake his hand. "I don't know where I'd be without you."

Before he can reply, Magda and Kat appear in the doorway, with Josh still tucked against her side. She must be exhausted from holding him, but I know there's no prying him away from her right now.

"Josh ate a snack," she says softly. "But he's very tired, and I think we need to get him settled in somewhere. Can we go now?"

"Yes, Katya." I offer her a pained smile. "We can go."

KAT TESTS the water in the bathtub with her fingers, her face heavy with exhaustion as Josh wiggles around in her grasp. She can barely hold him at this point, but I know she's trying to keep a sense of normalcy for him.

"I had a bath already," Josh protests, his bottom lip quivering. "I want to watch TV."

"You did have a bath this morning." Kat glances at his clothes and cringes at the blood that's been transferred from her. "But you need another one."

A slamming door down the hall in the hotel causes Kat to flinch. Josh cranes his neck to look up at her, his tiny hand coming up to her face. "What's wrong, Mommy?"

She chokes back a sob, and I gather Josh up into my arms, pulling Kat up beside me. "Mommy is very tired. She's going to go rest while I get you cleaned up. Okay, buddy?"

Josh still doesn't seem sold on the idea, and Kat already has a protest on her lips. But I need her to understand that she isn't doing things alone anymore. This might be the biggest clusterfuck of her life, but it's mine too. We're in this together.

"Just go sit down," I tell her. "Grab a drink from the minibar. Eat something, please. I've got this."

When it dawns on her that she's too tired to argue, she nods and pads out of the bathroom. A minute later, the television turns on, and I turn my attention to Josh. The first order of business is disposing of these clothes, but luckily for us, Talia was kind enough to give us a few of her son's outfits to see us through until I can buy some more.

I rifle through the bag, finding a pair of pajamas and hold them up for Josh to examine. "What do you think?"

"Minions?" He smiles his approval. "I like Minions."

I strip him down, and after a few more feeble protests, I get him into the bathwater. While I was terrified this morning that Josh would never calm down, it seems he's starting to get back to his normal self. Other than picking up on Kat's emotions, his main concerns right now are comfort and cartoons. He's young, and I can only hope that the events of today will be long forgotten over the coming weeks, but I have no way of knowing that.

After I get Josh washed up, I drain the tub and start a new bath while I dry him off with a towel.

"Another bath?" His face pinches in concern.

I chuckle as I kneel before him and help him into his pajamas. "That's for Mommy."

"So, I can watch TV now?" he pleads.

"Yes, you can watch a little TV now."

When he slips his hand in mine, something in my chest gives way. It feels like a brick wall with twenty years of repressed emotion crumbling under the weight of this one simple gesture.

My son.

It's still difficult to wrap my head around the fact that I'm a father. And right now, at this moment, I want more than anything for him to understand that. Whatever happens, I will protect him. I will take care of him. Even if that means going to war with Vasily.

Kat opens her eyes when we enter the room, stirring to life from the chair she's curled into. Her clothes are still a mess, and I know she needs to rest, but I also know she's desperate to wash the day off her.

I help Josh onto the bed, and she watches him as he settles onto his stomach and focuses on the singing dogs on TV. Within about two seconds, he's zoned out, and I'm in front of Kat, helping her up.

"What are we doing?" She protests.

"Getting you cleaned up."

"But Josh—"

"Josh will be okay right here. And we'll leave the bathroom door open so you can hear him, all right?"

It takes her a minute to nod her acceptance, but when I lead her into the bathroom, she attempts to start stripping off her clothes. Her limbs are too weak, and she can barely muster the energy, so I stop her, pausing to kiss her forehead and pull her against my chest. When I do, she chokes back a sob at the first glimpse of comfort she's had all day.

"It's okay, Katya. I've got you now."

Silent tears spill against my chest as I cradle her against me, and this time, I don't ask her to hold back. She lets it all out, until there's nothing left, and still we stand there. I pet her hair, rub her back, kiss her face. A reassuring presence is all I can be for her right now. This morning, I failed her. She probably doesn't trust me to tell her I won't let it happen again, but right now, I'm all she has.

"Everything is going to be okay," I whisper in her ear. "Just let me take care of you."

Slowly, I strip off her clothes, piece by piece, until she's naked before me. On any other occasion, I would already be balls deep inside her. But right now, that isn't what she needs. So instead, I help her into the bath and kneel beside the tub, using the detachable showerhead to begin the process of washing her body. At this moment, she's never looked so small. So fragile. My eyes absorb every detail of her skin, with my fingers following. I almost lost this today. That sinks in, over and over again, every second worse than the last. I'm trying not to think about it when I touch the birthmark on the back of her neck.

"Josh has the same one," I croak.

Kat nods. "I know."

She shivers when my soapy hands skate over her shoulders and down to her chest, grazing her nipples. Even when she's bruised and bloodied, she's still the most beautiful woman I've ever seen.

I wash her hair, massaging her scalp and her shoulders, and then rinse it all off before draining and refilling the tub once more with clean water. As she relaxes back against the porcelain wall, my fingers slip between her thighs, and her eyes open at half-mast.

"Don't worry," I tell her. "He can't see in here."

Her eyes fall shut again, and I drag my fingers over her clit, slowly massaging her there while she shudders, biting back her pleasure. It isn't sexual. It's just intimate. A way to release some of her emotions and allow her to fully relax. And as I bring her to climax, I'm satisfied that I've done my job when she bucks against me, her breath hissing between her teeth.

She's emotionally and physically spent as I gather her into my arms and towel her off, wrapping her in the hotel's bathrobe before I lay her on the bed beside Josh. She looks up at me, murmuring that she doesn't want me to go anywhere, and then falls back asleep.

3

LEV

Kat stirs from her sleep a little after midnight, blinking as she bolts upright in the bed. When her eyes collide with mine across the room, her shoulders relax, and she drags in a deep breath.

"How long have I been asleep?" she whispers.

"For a few hours."

I shut the brown paper file on the table in front of me, and her gaze moves to the bombshell I'm not quite ready to deliver just yet.

"What is that?"

I lean back against the chair and crane my neck to the side, attempting to relieve some of the tension that's gathered there. "I asked Alexei to do some research into the names listed on the drive. He's handing it off to me as he goes through it."

Kat frowns, glancing at Josh and adjusting his covers before she slips off the bed and comes to sit across from me. The soft glow of a lamp provides the only light in the hotel room, but I can still see the tension in her eyes.

"So, what happens now?" She swallows. "We can't hide out in this hotel forever."

"No, we can't," I agree. "I'm trying to figure out the next steps. And I know it's not fair for me to ask, but I need you to trust me right now, Katya."

Her fingers tangle together in her lap, and she seems to consider that before she makes her own suggestion. "Or we could just run, Lev. We could run to another city and never look back. Farther than Boston. We could go anywhere. California. Texas. A place where none of this exists."

I lean forward and wrap my fingers around hers, tugging her up and onto my lap. She relaxes into my chest, curling her legs between mine.

"Running isn't an option, sweetheart." I stroke her arm and bury my face into her neck. "I think you already know that. The only way to fix this is to face it head-on."

"Are you talking about going to war with Vasily?" she croaks.

"I don't know yet." My grip on her tightens. "But if that's what it comes down to—"

"You have a family now," she bites out. "That's

what you keep telling me. Your job is to protect us. To stay with us."

When her voice fractures, I drag my lips up to hers. "Shh, baby. I know."

We're both quiet for a while, lost in our own thoughts, before Kat speaks again.

"Is Andrei the one who killed Nina?"

"Yes."

"Then I'm glad he's dead," she whispers.

"Me too." I close my eyes and breathe her in.

While I might be glad that the world is rid of Andrei, I'm also aware of the shitstorm his death will rain down on us. And I think it's time that Kat understands that too. Going forward, I need her to be strong. I need her to trust that I'm doing what's necessary, even if she may not like it.

"I know you have some questions. Perhaps now is the time to ask them."

She looks up at me, curious, and I think... relieved. "Will you be honest with me?"

"Yes."

She grazes her fingers over my forearm, the smallest gesture of affection, and I don't even think she realizes she's doing it. But I do. And it means more than she could ever know.

"Is Vasily the head of your mafia family?" she asks.

"No. He's what you would call a captain, if you

will. He controls men beneath him, but he also reports to someone else."

"So he's powerful," she notes. "But he answers to someone else. Does that mean the man in charge will want us dead too?"

"Not likely," I tell her. "I doubt he's even aware of what's happening right now. Of course, Andrei's death might raise some questions, but Vasily isn't going to bring this to his boss. He handles things like this on his own, often under the radar of official Vor business. He'd have to be pretty desperate to take this all the way to the top."

Kat turns to study me. "How did you even get into this life?"

"It wasn't a conscious choice," I say. "My mother was killed when I was fifteen. My father was already gone. Vasily was the only family I had left. He took me in, and I became indebted to him for that. The rest... it just happened."

"But there must be a reason you've stayed all these years," she presses. "If you don't even like him."

I scratch at the stubble on my jaw and shake my head. "We have a complicated relationship. I don't think I ever really trusted him, but I felt I owed him. And I did respect him at one time. But whatever loyalty I may have had for him is gone now."

I intentionally leave out the part about my

mother, deciding it best for now not to mention it to Kat. At least not until this is over. I don't want her to doubt my motivations.

"So, if you are his nephew, then what does that make you?" she asks. "How do you fit into the mafia?"

"Officially? I don't." I shrug. "Vasily never asked me to be inducted. I think he liked having his own control over me. I am connected only through him."

"And Alexei," she observes.

"He is my cousin. And yes, he is also a Vor, but he is a good man. We can trust him."

"Can I trust you?"

Her question robs the breath from my lungs.

"I am here to protect you now, sweetheart. Please don't ever doubt that."

"But those weren't always your intentions," she argues. "Andrei said you were supposed to kill me."

My jaw flexes, and her eyes feel like they are penetrating deep into my soul as she waits for me to explain this to her.

"I was sent to kill you," I confirm. "But I didn't. Because the moment I saw you again, I fucking knew, even before Josh, that you were meant to be mine."

"How can I trust that?" she chokes out. "If you even considered it—"

"Because I would sooner put a bullet in my own

head, Katya." I force her back against me when she tries to pull away. "I'm in this now. Don't you understand? I've left everything behind. I betrayed my blood. I killed my own cousin. And I would do it all again to protect this life I'm building with you."

She falls quiet, and I still don't know if she trusts my intentions, but regardless, she doesn't try to leave me again.

"What are we supposed to do until you figure everything out?"

"For now, we'll stay here," I tell her. "Tomorrow, we will try to make things as normal as we can for Josh. We'll grab some more clothes, food, whatever we need. And when I hear back from Alexei, we will start planning, okay?"

She tilts her head up to meet my gaze, and for the first time all day, she looks like some of her strength is returning. "I'm putting my trust in you, Lev. Please don't let us down."

4

KAT

The following morning, I watch Josh as he digs into the pancakes Lev brought him from the McDonald's down the road. He eats them with a voracious appetite, and I remember we didn't really have more than that snack at Lev's cousin's house last night.

"McDonald's is a treat for him," I tell Lev who is watching him with that same expression of awe and pride. And right now, a little wincing as Josh maneuvers a sticky piece of pancake dripping with syrup into his mouth, not quite getting it to its destination directly as it drops onto the open palm of the hand he's holding beneath his plastic fork.

"Wow," Lev says.

I have to chuckle as he takes in Josh licking the syrup off his palm.

"Is it driving you nuts?" I ask him, appreciating this moment of levity. Of almost normal. "I mean, you're kind of a neat freak."

He turns to me. "A little, but he's cute. And I'm not a neat freak. I just like things organized and in their place."

"Well, welcome to fatherhood."

Fatherhood.

We both stop at my comment and just look at each other.

Lev reaches out a hand and brushes my hair back from my forehead, touching the bruise there.

"I wouldn't change anything when it comes to him and you. I mean the part with us. Our family."

I shift my gaze to the cup of coffee in my hands, smiling because I feel the same way. But at the same time, I know there's the other part. The Russian mafia part.

As if on cue, his phone rings. We both have the new ones his cousin Alexei arranged for us. I don't know Alexei, and a part of me questions whether he can be trusted. If he doesn't have a way of tracking those phones and telling Vasily of our location. But Lev trusts him and even as fucked up as his family is, I see that level of trust between him and Alexei. I saw it with Pasha, too.

I don't trust most people. Nina was the one who

knew the most about me, but even she didn't know everything.

Joshua knew. Joshua lived it with me. But he died, and after his death, I learned to keep my secrets.

But I told Lev the other night. I told him more than I've ever told anyone, and it felt natural. It felt good to say some of those things out loud.

Secrets hold power over you, and in a way, when you speak them out loud and tell them to another human being, it gives you your power back. I didn't realize that until the other night.

I look up at Lev. He's distracted, expression serious as he talks into his phone in Russian. And when I go to him and hug him, he's surprised. I know it in the break in his sentence. In that moment, he hesitates before wrapping his arm around me. I see it in the way he looks at me when I pull back.

"Mommy?" Josh is standing behind me hands palm-up. "I'm sticky."

I watch Lev walk into the small attached living room part of our accommodation.

"Shocker," I say, putting my coffee down and walking him into the bathroom to wash his hands. He still doesn't quite reach the sink easily, so after rolling up his sleeves, I lift him and balance him on one leg as I wash his little hands.

"Can we go home now?" he asks.

When I look up from his hands, I find his eyes on me in the mirror, and inside them, I see the residue of the events of the past twenty-four hours.

"Not yet, sweetheart. We're going to take a vacation with Lev first." I don't want to lie to him, but I need him to keep feeling secure and safe. At least as much as possible.

"But I want to go home."

I switch off the water and busy myself with drying his hands, then crouch down to talk to him.

"You were scared yesterday, weren't you?"

His eyes grow glassy with tears, and he nods.

"That man was a bad man, Josh, but he's gone now, and he can't hurt you anymore, okay?"

He touches my face, the spot on my forehead I thought I'd covered up so well with my hair.

"What about you? Can he hurt you?"

I take his hand and kiss the inside of it, then hug him. "No, sweetheart, he can't hurt anyone ever again."

Lev knocks on the door that I'd left ajar, pushing it open all the way.

I straighten, keeping hold of Josh's hand, and watch Lev process what he sees. I study him, seeing how tightly his jaw is set and the furrow between his eyebrows.

"Pasha's doing well," he says, then turns to Josh.

"He said he'll be making you marshmallow pancakes again in no time."

I look down to see Josh smile, and he's just a normal little kid again. "I love marshmallow pancakes."

We walk back out into the bedroom where Lev switches on a cartoon for Josh.

"Pasha's really okay?" I ask.

"Yes. He wanted to make sure you knew, and he also apologized."

"Apologized? For what? He almost died for us."

"He wanted you to know he felt bad about leaving you and Josh to go to the hardware store."

"I hope you told him not to be silly."

"I did. But he's right. He shouldn't have left you."

"Lev—"

"We need to discuss other things, though." His expression darkens. "Where's your new phone?"

"In my purse," I tell him, getting it out of my bag. I hadn't even looked at it. This is the one Alexei had given to Lev. "Here." I hand it to him.

Lev takes it, fingers quick as he types something in, then holds it out to me. "I just programmed Alexei's private number." He holds up the contact under AX. "If anything happens to me—"

"What?"

"If anything happens to me, or we get separated, or you can't get in touch with me for any reason, you call him. He's the only one you call. Do you understand?"

"We're not going to get separated. Nothing's going to happen to you."

"Shh." He glances at Josh. "I don't want Josh getting upset."

"But—"

"Just a precaution. That's all. Nothing is going to happen to me, Kat."

I take the phone and push it into my back pocket.

"Is everything okay? Did something happen on your call? Is there something new and that's why—"

"We need to get on the road. I want to put more distance between us and Vasily. I'm going to run to the store and buy some things we need." He gestures to my hair. "You'll need to color your hair. It's too recognizable."

I touch my hair. "Josh is used to me like this. I don't think we should change—"

"The important thing is to keep Josh safe, and that means to keep out of sight. We'll find a way to explain it."

"He wants to go home."

"Yeah, well, he can't do that right now, and neither can you, so stay focused, Katerina." This is a different side to Lev from the tender one of last night and the fatherly one of this morning. This is the sharper, edgier side. And I realize something. Something I've known all along but never consciously acknowledged.

He's a trained killer.

He watches me as I think this, and I know he knows what's going on in my head. I see it on his face. But he doesn't try to soothe me or fill my head with pretty, meaningless words. This is reality. He and I both know it.

"Did you only talk to Pasha?" I know he didn't. I heard him say Alexei's name, and I get the feeling he heard something he didn't like.

"No, I spoke with my cousin too."

"Did something else happen? You seem more anxious."

"Of course, I'm anxious, Kat. How do you expect me to be?" he snaps but catches himself, shaking his head. "I'm sorry."

"What did he tell you?"

"What do you need me to pick up for Josh at the store?" he asks instead of answering my question, and something in his expression tells me I'm on to something.

"Um...he has some clothes from Talia but probably needs some more things, jeans and sweaters, underwear, socks. And maybe some toys? Just some trucks or toy cars. Do you remember the cereal he likes?"

Lev nods. "What about you? What do you need?"

"Nothing I can think of. Well, maybe...Can't we come with you?"

"It's better if you stay here. They'll be looking for the three of us."

Shit. I knew this, didn't I?

"What do you need me to pick up?"

"Tampons."

He nods, and if he's uncomfortable, he doesn't let on. Instead, he walks me into the bathroom and closes the door. From the back of the waistband of his jeans and under his shirt, he pulls out a small pistol and holds it in the palm of his hand.

I back up a step and shake my head.

"It's not exactly the same model you pulled on me but similar enough."

"I don't want that."

He steps closer, puts the pistol on the counter behind me and pulls me to him, rubbing my arms.

"You won't need it," he says, "but I'd feel better if you had it while I'm not here."

My heart is racing. "I don't like this."

"I like it even less, but if you have to use it, use it. Do not hesitate. Do you understand me?"

"I—"

"You hesitated with me. It takes a split second for a man to overpower you. You know that. Do not hesitate. Do you understand?"

I nod.

He takes the pistol, giving me a quick tutorial, but it's almost exactly the same as the one I had. He then tucks it into the back of my jeans and pulls my sweater over it to keep it out of sight.

"I'll be as fast as I can. There's a store two blocks away. You lock the door behind me. No one knows we're here. As soon as I'm back, you'll color your hair, and then we're gone."

"Where are we going to go?"

"New York City."

"New York City? But isn't that closer to Vasily with him being in Philadelphia? Wouldn't we be in more danger there?"

He sighs. "I'll explain later. Let me get to the store. The sooner we leave here, the better."

5

KAT

I lock the door after Lev leaves and watch him through the window of the second-floor hotel room as he looks around the almost empty parking lot, then gets into the SUV. Before he closes the door, he looks up at me. We stay like that for a long minute before he drives off.

In the bedroom, Josh is sitting against the pillows with Wally in his hands, rubbing the little stuffed animal's well-worn ear, his attention wholly absorbed by the cartoon.

I'm about to go sit beside him when I see Lev's duffel bag tucked behind the chair by the small table.

Glancing once more at Josh, I go to it, pick it up, and carry it into the other room. I set it on the couch, and as I unzip it, I tell myself I'm just going to look through what we have packed for Josh.

What I see first is a set of neatly folded clothes for Lev and me, and several more sets for Josh. I smile when I find the coloring book and crayons. That was thoughtful.

Pushing those aside, I find a small box. It's older and decidedly ornate. Not like Lev's taste at all. I pick it out of the bag and look at the intricate wood carving and realize it's old. An antique trinket box.

Curious, I open it and gasp.

Glancing through the open door of the bedroom, I'm relieved Josh hasn't heard me, and return my attention to the box of jewelry. Rings and bracelets and emeralds and diamonds all set in gold like the kind you'd find in high-end antique shops. They're beautiful. And I wonder what Lev is doing with them when I pick up the locket.

The closure is stuck, so I have to set the box down to try to open it. It's very delicate, and it takes me a few tries, but when I get it open, my heart stops.

I peer closer at the little photos inside. There are two.

One is of a family—a man, a woman and a baby. I can see the woman's warm smile even in the tiny photograph, and it makes me smile to see it. The man's face is more blurred, and the baby I really can't see more than the bundle of blankets.

But it's not that one that has my heart skip a beat. It's the other one.

The little boy. It could be Josh.

Was this Lev's mother? Are these her jewels?

"Mommy," comes Josh's sleepy voice from inside.

I startle, feeling like I've been caught doing something I shouldn't be doing. I get up, setting the box on the sofa. I go to him. "Yes, baby?"

"*Blue's Clues* is next." He smiles and lays his head down, putting his thumb in his mouth.

"You love *Blue's Clues*." I tuck him in under the blankets as his eyes droop. I kiss his forehead. "I love you."

He doesn't answer as the theme song to the cartoon comes on, and he focuses back on the TV.

I return to the outer room, pulling the bedroom door almost all the way closed behind me. I don't want to close it fully in case Josh calls to me.

Sitting down on the couch, I mean to put the locket away, but when I do, I see something else. The folder Lev was looking at. The one he closed when I got close to him.

My heartbeat accelerates as I take hold of it. I shouldn't look. I should ask him to show me. But my hands are moving to lift it out, and I set it on my lap and don't hesitate to open it.

And when I do, when I see what's inside, I feel a sudden chill. My hands get clammy and blood pounds against my ears, and I don't even hear the lock click. I don't hear him as he walks in because I'm staring down at the photo in the folder. The photo of the woman with red hair and light green eyes and the biggest smile I've ever seen.

My mother.

She must have been eighteen or nineteen when this was taken. She was so beautiful. I had a smaller one just like it a long time ago, but after I was taken in by the Georges, it disappeared. They denied having taken it, of course, and I lost that last piece of my mother.

Seeing it now, bigger, not wrinkled or worn, seeing her smiling like this, well, it makes my heart hurt.

"What are you doing, Katerina?"

I jump with an audible yelp, and the folder slips off my lap, pages scattering to the floor.

Lev stands there, leather jacket zipped up, two plastic bags in one hand and keys in the other. He looks at the papers on the floor, then at the trinket box, then at me.

Without a word, he walks to the bedroom, peeks inside, then closes the door.

That clicking makes me sit up a little taller as I turn to face him.

Lev walks back toward me, setting the bags on a chair and the keys on the table. His eyes move over the trinket box as he unzips his jacket and takes it off, then sets his gun on the table.

His is bigger than the one he gave me. It's the one he used to kill Andrei, and he's very well equipped to handle it.

"Where's the pistol I gave you?" he asks, stepping closer.

I reach behind me to take it out of the waistband of my jeans and hand it to him.

He puts it beside his on the table, and all I can think is we're quite the couple. Bonnie and Clyde.

"We should hide those. What if Josh—"

"Josh is asleep. I asked you a question."

I look at the papers on the floor. "I have a right to know what's going on." I stand, then step to him to face-off. "I have a right to know what you're doing with a file on my mother."

He studies me, cocks his head to the side, and steps toward me, closing those last few feet of space.

"It's my responsibility to keep you and our son safe. I will make the call on what you see when. I decide what information you need, when you need it."

"I'm not the little woman you keep barefoot and pregnant in the kitchen, Lev. I won't ever be that. What are you doing with this? Why do you have it?

And what does my mother have to do with any of this?"

"We'll discuss it later. When you're ready."

"You don't get to decide when I'm ready. My mother—"

"We will discuss it later when we can talk." He rubs my arms, his touch not quite as gentle as he can be. "Our son is sleeping in the next room."

"Our son that I've been raising on my own for three years. That I've kept safe for three years."

"What are you saying?" He drops his arms.

"Nothing." I shift my gaze.

"You think you were safe?" he asks.

"Well..." I falter.

When he takes another step, I match his, going backward. But I should know better because one more, and my back is to the wall. It's exactly where he wants me because in the next instant, he has my arms stretched over my head and my wrists pinned to the wall.

"Lev—"

"You weren't safe, Katerina. You were never safe. You hid well, I'll give you that, but I found you and Vasily's men followed the day we left. I've told you more than once that I will keep you safe. I've asked you to trust me, and I think my actions have proven that I have yours and Josh's best interests at heart."

"But—"

"You need to trust that I will tell you what I can when I can."

"My mother—"

"You want me to tell you about your mother?"

Something in his eyes tells me I don't want to know, but the thing is, I *need* to know. No matter how terrible it is, and it is terrible because there's no other reason he'd have a file on my mother. I *need* to know.

"That accident that killed her, Kat, it doesn't appear to have been an accident at all."

"What?"

"Not what you expected or hoped to hear?"

"What are you talking about?"

"Someone wanted her dead, and the fact that she was on Vasily's list tells me it was him."

"I don't understand."

"Fuck."

He lets go of my wrists and walks away, running a hand through his hair.

"What does my mother have to do with Vasily or any of this?"

He turns back to me, looking me over. He comes toward me, and he's so close I have to crane my neck to look up at him.

"I care about you, Kat. Do you know that?"

"Tell me."

"I don't have anything to tell you that won't upset you. That's why I haven't said anything."

"You can't decide that for me."

He steps backward and sits on the sofa, hands on his knees. "This is a goddamn shitshow."

I move toward him, kneel between his legs, and put my hands on his thighs. I make him look at me.

"You said your mother was killed. Who killed her?" I suspect, but I guess a part of me can't believe blood would do that to blood. But that's stupid, isn't it? I mean, I saw what Lev did to Andrei. What Andrei was willing to do to Lev.

He sits back, one hand rubbing the back of his neck. He won't look at me.

"Lev?"

He turns to me, and there's such a deep sadness in his eyes that I feel it inside me. He scrubs his face, shaking his head.

"I don't know, Kat. It's just...it's fucked up. She didn't deserve what happened to her. She was a good woman. You would have liked her. And she would have liked you."

I lean up, take his face into my hands, and I kiss him. He doesn't respond at first, but he doesn't pull back either.

"I care about you too, you know?" I say.

He looks at me for a long minute, then pulls me to him and kisses me back. I slide my hands to the buckle of his belt and undo it. I unzip his jeans and slide my hand inside to grip his cock, stroking it, feeling it grow rigid in my hand as I watch his pupils dilate and his eyes darken.

His breathing becomes shorter, and I feel my own need. But then he closes his hand over mine to pull me off. "Katya, now isn't the time."

"Now is the time. We need this. Both of us."

He loosens his hold on me.

Leaning forward, I first lick my lips then the glistening head of his cock before taking him into my mouth. I keep my eyes on him, and he watches me as I take him.

He closes his hand over the back of my head and pulls me to him.

"Fuck, Katya." He draws me closer, fisting my hair as he drags me over him, pushing deeper until I can't take anymore, then easing back, drawing me far enough back to look at me, then repeating, going deeper.

Abruptly, he pulls me off him and reaches to undo my jeans. Pushing them and my panties roughly off, he draws me onto his lap.

I straddle him, closing my eyes as I take his length inside me. He kisses me, and with his hands on my hips, he moves me over him. One hand cups the back of my head, fingers digging into my scalp as the other closes over my shoulder, gripping hard as he pushes deeper. He kisses me all the while, mouth to my mouth, tongue on my tongue as we make love like this, him bare inside me, him thickening inside me as his thrusts grow more hurried. He lifts me, flipping us over so I'm on the couch and he's between my legs, buried inside me.

I cry out when I come, and he closes his mouth over mine, swallowing my cry as he moans with his final thrust. When he stills, I feel him come, feel the pulsing throbbing of his cock as he empties inside me, and when he's finished, when we're spent, he drops his head to my neck, forehead sweaty with the effort as I cling to him and listen to our matching breaths as they slowly return to normal.

He turns his face to watch me and brushes the hair that's sticking to my forehead back.

I told him I care about him. He told me the same. But it's so much more than that. God. So much more.

"We'll talk, okay? I'll tell you what I can, but just trust me to do it on my own time."

The TV goes off inside, and we're both up in an instant. Lev tucks himself back into his jeans and I pull on my underwear and jeans. He sweeps both guns off the table to tuck mine into the duffel and his into the waistband of his jeans.

"Mommy?" comes Josh's voice as the door opens. He stands there, rubbing his eyes.

"Hey kiddo, look what I got you." Lev opens one

of the bags and pulls out a copy of *Good Night, Gorilla*.

Josh runs toward him, arms out to take the book. "Mine?"

"Yours."

He hugs Josh, and Josh lays his head on Lev's shoulder as he clutches the book and smiles. I smile too, watching our little family.

Lev turns to me then, opening the bag to take out the box of hair dye. Black.

Although reluctant, I take it from him. I know he's right. I have to do this.

He draws me to him so he's hugging us both and kisses my forehead. "I'm going to miss the red," he says.

6

LEV

Katerina flips to the last page of *Good night, Gorilla*, quieting her voice as she peeks over her shoulder to check on Josh. At the same time, I glance at him in the rearview mirror, and relax a little as she confirms that he's asleep.

"It's good for him to keep a consistent naptime," she says. "If nothing else."

"It won't always be this way." I reach over and tuck a strand of black hair behind her ear. She looks different but still beautiful. Always beautiful.

"I know." She glances out the window and shrugs. "Inevitably, something will have to change."

I don't want to worry her, so I don't bring up the fact that things have already changed and not for the better. During my call with Alexei this morning, he informed me that Andrei is, by some miracle, still alive.

I guess I shouldn't have unloaded four of the shots into his dick. Being the fucking oaf that he is, it shouldn't surprise me. He could be hit by a bus and still probably manage to crawl out from beneath it. But if there's one small comfort in all of this, it's that he'll certainly never fuck anything else again.

In addition to that fucking cockroach, Alexei also informed me that Vasily is losing his shit. He's already sent out at least a dozen of his soldiers to look for us. Word is he's been combing every Vory safe house on the East Coast as we speak, and he's already paid two visits to Alexei's home.

Alexei was quick to let me know that Vasily was practically foaming at the mouth. He's never seen him like this. The words homicidal lunatic were uttered more than once during that conversation. He has it out for me, and he especially wants Kat. My cousin didn't sugarcoat any of the details. Vasily is out for blood, and there is no going back now.

I've started a war with one of the most powerful men in Philadelphia. Vasily has many contacts. Government agents in his pockets. Cops. Politicians. The list is endless. They are all fucking terrified of him for this very reason. But when I glance at Kat riding shotgun beside me, I know that whatever comes next will be worth it. I will burn Vasily's whole fucking world if that's what it takes to keep my family together. If he wants to come for us, I will be the one to come for him instead. I will not rest until I have destroyed his life and taken as much as he's taken from me.

As for Andrei, he might be alive for now, but he better enjoying every goddamn breath he's granted because they are certainly numbered.

"Are we going to another hotel in New York?" Kat asks, breaking through my thoughts.

"Yes. But we'll have to stop and stay the night somewhere in between."

She gives me a questioning glance but thinks better of asking me why. The drive from Boston to New York City is only a few hours, but there are three different addresses I need to check out along the way. Alexei could only speculate on Maxim's location, but he suspects that he's been hiding out with his ex-girlfriend all these years, and her family has ties to Rhode Island and Connecticut.

When we stop in Providence a little over an hour later, Kat doesn't think to question it. I drive around for a while before settling on a hotel downtown. It's only when we're inside the room that Kat seems to relax.

"Can we afford to keep staying in places like this?" she asks.

"Don't worry about it, sweetheart." I kiss her on

the forehead and squeeze her ass in my palm. "We can afford it."

She chews on her lip and gets Josh settled at the coffee table with a coloring book and some crayons. I rifle through the duffel and grab some ammo, and she frowns when I stuff it into my jacket.

"What are you doing?"

"I have to go out for a while. It might be a few hours. Can you hold everything down here?"

She doesn't seem entirely sure of that, but I give her a long lingering kiss to try to make her forget her nerves. It seems to work, and when she looks up at me with heavy-lidded eyes, she curls her fingers into mine.

"Or you could just stay here for a while."

A grin tugs at my lips as I cup her face and kiss her one more time. "If I could, I would, but this is important. I'll be back, but just remember what I said about Alexei. In the meantime, I'll be texting you often to check in on you."

"Okay." She squares her shoulders and nods. "But isn't there something I could be doing here to help? I'm sick of just laying low and watching TV. If I can help you, Lev, then let me."

I consider her offer and decide that if nothing else, it can't hurt. Grabbing the pad and pen from the desk, I hand it to her.

"If you want to help, write down everything you

remember about your mother. Her family. Places she may have lived. Anything she may have said to you. I know you were young, but any detail you might remember could be important."

"But why?" She frowns. "I don't understand what she has to do with any of this."

I sigh, really not wanting to get into this with her right now. But I know she's not going to relent until I throw her a bone. At least a little bit at a time, so she can process everything slowly.

"When I spoke to Alexei this morning, he mentioned that your mother had a connection to Gleb Mikhailov. Have you ever heard that name before?"

"No." She shrugs. "Who is he?"

"He's one of the Vory crime bosses. A big one. And he's a very powerful man."

Kat swallows, her expression morphing to one of horror. "You think my mother was connected to the mob?"

"It's looking that way," I admit. "But I'm trying to figure out how."

Kat sits down on the sofa and shakes her head. "So, her car accident..."

"It could have been a mob hit," I finish for her. "But I don't know yet. That's why this is important. Anything you can think of might help."

She leans back into the sofa and blows out a breath. "I'll see what I can remember."

"Good girl." I lean down and kiss her again, my tongue invading her mouth, and for a minute, I'm tempted to stay behind after all. But I know that I can't. If Maxim gets even a hint that someone is sniffing around for him, he'll disappear before I even get close.

"I'll be back." I pull away reluctantly. "Take care of our boy."

"I will." Kat offers me a dazed smile. "We'll be waiting for you."

AFTER SITTING OUTSIDE of the first address for an hour, I quickly come to the conclusion that this isn't where Maxim is hiding out. The house is owned by his ex-girlfriend's father, but so far, all I've seen are an older couple and a bunch of rug rats running around the place.

I text Kat to check in, and she responds promptly as I drive to the second location. It's a run-down single-level home squatting in the Elmwood neighborhood, and while it isn't the place I'd choose to call home if I could help it, it definitely looks more like Maxim's speed.

For two hours, I stare at the peeling paint and

front yard full of weeds. At first glance, it doesn't even look like anyone actually lives here. But there's a garbage bin on the sidewalk and letters in the mailbox.

The problem is, I can't stay camped out here all day. It's past five already, and I don't want to leave Kat and Josh alone for much longer. At the very least, I need to be back by bedtime.

I grab my phone and pull up a Google search for some local bars in the neighborhood. If there's one thing I know about Maxim, it's that he likes his whiskey. I doubt that's changed. The man was a sloppy fucking drunk.

It's the only lead I have to follow as I drive around the area, scoping out a few of the local bars. The first three turn up nothing, and I'm already considering it a lost cause. But there's one more on the list, and when I pull into the parking lot, it seems like exactly the kind of place where he'd hang out. It's barely a shack. A business hanging on by the skin of its teeth in a city that depends on drunks like Maxim to keep it afloat.

I park the SUV and walk inside, and every head at the bar turns to study me when I take a seat. As I suspected, these are all locals. The beer is cheap, and the stale peanut shells on the floor feel like home to many of them. But I don't see Maxim. At least, not right away.

The bartender asks me what I want, and I tell her nothing. When I stand to leave, that's when I see the bathroom door swinging open down the hallway. It's not a well-lit area, so I can't make out the guy's face until he stumbles into the glow of one of the neon signs. Just about the same time recognition sparks in my brain, he notices me, and the sneaky bastard pivots on his heel and bolts back down the hallway.

Son of a bitch.

I don't know if anyone else has even noticed, but right now, I can't be fucked with worrying about that as I take off after him. He slips out the rear exit door, and it slams shut in my face before I reach it. He's ten, maybe fifteen steps ahead of me when I stumble out into the alley and catch him sliding around the corner.

It's dark, and I can't see for shit when I go after him. But I don't have to see to know the sound I just heard was him cocking a gun.

"I don't want to shoot you, Lev." His voice is the only proof that it's actually him. In the dark, I can barely make out his form huddled near the dumpster.

"Then don't," I tell him. "I'm not here to fuck up your life. I just want to talk."

"Fucking talk," he snorts. "Right. Is that what Vasily told you to say? And I'm supposed to swallow that bullshit?"

"I'm not here for Vasily." I take another hesitant step forward. "I'm here because of Vasily."

"Step the fuck off," he clips out. "Or I'll blow your goddamn brains out. I don't care."

"You know me, Maxim." I sigh. "You've known me since I was practically a kid. All I'm asking for is a few minutes. One conversation. Then I'll leave here, and you'll never have to see me again. Vasily will never know."

"Sorry, kid," he murmurs. "But whatever bullshit you're trying to sell me today, I ain't buying. I know he wants me dead. I'm not stupid—"

"He wants me dead too."

A cavernous wall of silence fills the space between us as he digests my confession. Honestly, I don't know if there's anything I can say at this point to make him believe me. He's been on the run for years, constantly looking over his shoulder. I'm sure the paranoia is getting to him, and I can't blame him for that. I've only been at it for a few days, and I already feel like I'm losing my goddamn mind.

"He wants to kill the mother of my son." I force the words out. "Maybe my son too. Fuck if I know. It's just me against his army. I started a fucking war, and I don't know if I'll even survive the week. That's why I'm here. I need your help."

For a few long seconds, he doesn't answer me. And I'm dead certain he's going to tell me to fuck off again, but instead, he steps out into the light and gestures me back into the alleyway.

"Show me proof. I'm not going to listen to anything you tell me without proof."

"Proof?" I repeat.

Christ. What the fuck can I show him?

Slowly, I retrieve the phone from my pocket, careful not to make any quick moves. Maxim watches me with calloused eyes and a face that's aged well beyond his years. He's only in his mid-fifties, but he looks closer to seventy right now.

"This is a picture of my son." I turn the phone screen so he can see it. "And this is his mother. Hopefully, one day, my wife. If we survive this week."

"Those could be anybody." He shrugs. "Sorry, kid, but I can't help you."

"You can talk to her," I tell him. "Just give me a second."

Maxim watches me carefully as I dial Kat. To my relief, she answers on the second ring.

"Lev, is everything okay?"

"Yes, sweetheart." I turn on the speakerphone. "I'm here with an old friend. And I just need you to do something for me, okay? I need you to tell him in your own words what happened with Vasily."

The other end of the line is quiet for a pause until she releases a breath. "Are you sure this is safe?"

"It is," I answer. "Please, just tell him. Everything in your own words."

Kat comes through for me, starting slowly. Explaining how we met. How she got pregnant and went on the run. How I found her, and then everything imploded. Inevitably, her story leads back to everything that happened at the safe house in Philly. When she's done, she wraps it all up with a simple sentence. "And that's pretty much where we're at now."

Maxim is quiet, and I can't read his expression. But I'm hoping that he'll believe Kat, even if he can't believe me.

"I'm going to hang up now," I tell her. "I'll be back a little later, okay?"

"Lev." Her voice fractures. "Please be careful."

"I will," I assure her. "We'll be back together before you know it."

We both end the call, and I move my attention back to Maxim. He reeks of whiskey, but despite that, he seems to have his faculties in order.

"If what she says is true, it sounds like you've really gotten yourself into a bind, kid."

"It is true."

"Regardless"—he sighs—"I don't want to get involved. I left that world for a reason. I don't need you bringing trouble back to my doorstep."

"I just need some answers. Give me one hour,

and I'll fuck off out of your life and you'll never see me again."

"Sounds too good to be true." He laughs sourly. "Fucking Christ."

"You know me," I tell him. "I grieved for you. I believed you were dead. You were the only asshole in that place I liked."

Maxim scratches at his stubble and chuckles. "You better not make me fucking regret this, kid."

7

LEV

Maxim sits down in the recliner across from me, gun still clutched in his hand. We're back at his place, and the state of his affairs is even sadder than I originally would have thought. The house is mostly just an empty shell, and in that aspect, it reminds me of my own place back in Philly. I understand the concept. When you might have to pick up and leave everything behind at a moment's notice, there really isn't any point in collecting things.

"What happened between you and Vasily?" I ask.

"What did he tell you happened?" he challenges.

"Not a whole lot." I shrug. "He came back to the club one night, said you were dead, and I'd need to run some extra jobs for him. That was the extent of it. He's not exactly the kind of man you ask a lot of questions, as you know."

Maxim snorts. "Yeah, I do know. That was the fucking problem. I guess I just got sick of taking his orders. No explanations, no logic. I did what I was told for a long time, but when I started to ask questions, Vasily didn't like it. He likes his soldiers deaf, dumb, and blind."

"But you weren't," I hedge. "Did you see something you shouldn't have?"

He shakes his head. "You first, kid. This isn't a one-way street. You want me to trust you, there needs to be some give and take here."

I lean back into the sofa and consider where I should even fucking begin. Maxim isn't in a position to do any real damage to me at this stage of his life. He has no more connections in my world, so he wants me to give him some insurance, and that's understandable. But more than that, I'm hoping he will know something about what I have to tell him.

"A little over four years ago, Vasily asked me to do a job. He wanted me to keep an eye on one of his connections, William von Brandt. He said he'd been talking to the feds. We roughed him up a bit, gave him a warning, but William didn't listen. He stole a flash drive from Vasily, and shit hit the fan. I didn't know what was on it because we couldn't find it anywhere in the von Brandt house. But eventually, I got my hands on it, and I realized it was a list of names."

Maxim holds up a finger to stop me as he staggers into the kitchen and grabs a bottle of whiskey from the cupboard. When he returns to his chair, he offers it to me, and I shake my head.

"Now you've got my attention," he says. "Go on."

"The list has a lot of names. Most of them didn't mean anything to me. But I had a friend do some digging, and after connecting the dots, we realized that there was a neighbor in my mother's apartment building on that list. A cop too. Both were killed not long after her."

"It's a shame what happened to your mother." Maxim cringes as he takes a swig from the bottle.

"Andrei killed her."

"I know, kid."

I study him, waiting for him to say something else. It never occurred to me that Maxim would know about it, but it only makes sense. For as long as he worked for Vasily, he would have seen and heard a lot of shit.

"Were you there?" I clip out.

"Fuck no." He glares at me. "I don't run jobs on women, and Vasily knew that. After I fucked it up the first time, he never asked me again. I didn't even have any idea who you were until he brought you into the club. By then, your mother was already dead."

"What do you mean you fucked it up the first time?" I ask.

He rocks back and kicks his boot up onto his opposite knee, then takes another swig from the bottle and wipes his lips. "There was a woman. A long time ago. Vasily was using her as a pawn. She had an affair with Gleb Mikhailov and ran information back to Vasily. That arrangement worked out just fine until Vasily ran into some sort of complication with her. She tried to go into hiding, but Vasily found her a few years later. He wanted me to take care of it. But I didn't realize she had a kid. The second I saw that, I backed the fuck out. I couldn't do it. Regardless, it didn't matter. He had it done anyway."

I shake my head, trying to process what he's telling me. There's no way he could be talking about Kat's mother, but it's too similar to discount. The words are rushing from my lips before my mind can even catch up.

"Ciara March?"

Maxim's eyebrows shoot up. "How the hell did you know that?"

"Her name was on that list," I choke out. "At least we think it's supposed to be her name."

"I'll be damned," he murmurs. "I haven't heard that name in at least twenty years."

"The daughter." My throat is so dry, I can hardly get my thoughts out. "She was Gleb's?"

Maxim nods. "She was. Ciara told me that when I came for her. I think she still wasn't sure if she could trust me after I warned her away, and that was the only bargaining chip she had. Nobody in his right mind would hurt Gleb's kid, but the irony was that I don't think he ever knew she even existed."

My phone signals a text from Kat. She's getting worried, but there's still a lot to discuss with Maxim.

"Are you going to be around tomorrow?" I ask him as I tap out a message to Kat.

"Why?" he grumbles.

"I have someone I'd like you to meet."

He opens his mouth to protest, but I don't let him get that far.

"It's Ciara's daughter."

8

KAT

"Can we go to the playground, Mommy?"

Josh is getting bored of being cooped up indoors all day, and the allure of his unlimited TV time has worn off.

I check the time on my phone, refreshing it in the hopes of a message from Lev while I'm at it, but he's been quiet since his call a couple of hours ago.

"It's getting late for that, but I saw a Dairy Queen around the corner. Maybe we can walk over in a little bit and get some ice cream?" I want to wait until full dark, which will be very soon.

"Ice cream sundae?"

"Yep."

He smiles wide as he nods enthusiastically.

"You have to eat your dinner first, though," I tell

him, eyeing his half-eaten bowl of spaghetti which came from a can I warmed up in the kitchenette.

"All of it?"

"All of it."

He makes a face but picks up his spoon and starts to eat again.

I walk back to the desk and stare at the nearly blank sheet of paper.

Lev wanted me to write down everything I remembered about my mother, but what he suggested, that she was in some way involved with Vasily, it makes no sense. She can't have been.

Although there is one detail about the accident that killed her that always stood out to me.

I don't remember much about the few years I was with my mom, but I think that's pretty normal. I'm not sure at what age one begins to create memories—at least more than blips of scenes. And even those, I don't know if I made them up or if they truly happened.

Singing. I remember that. She had a pretty voice. And I remember her hair. I think it's the way Josh holds mine when he sleeps that makes me think of it. She had beautiful red hair.

But again, are they true memories or my brain creating history to fill in the empty spaces?

Red hair and a pretty singing voice. And maybe love.

That's not a memory, though. It's a feeling. I felt loved. Or maybe it's that I felt the absence of exactly that after she died and my time in foster care began that makes it so visceral a thing.

I got my hands on the police report once I was out of juvenile detention and legally an adult. There were photos of the scene, of the car, a simple little black Kia, something unremarkable, wrapped around a tree. There were white streaks around the driver's side door, and when I'd asked about them, the officer had said she'd probably been in another accident prior to that one. When I pushed for more, he admitted there wasn't any record of another accident, but that he wasn't surprised because my mother hadn't been insured, which would mean she probably wouldn't have reported a previous incident.

It had seemed strange, but I hadn't had any reason to question him further. The accident was fifteen years old and the case closed. Slippery conditions on mostly deserted roads. Period. The one officer I did manage to get ahold of who was at the scene had retired a few years earlier and only recalled what a pity he'd thought it for her to have died so young and how lucky it was that I'd survived.

Strangely enough, I'd only survived because my car seat wasn't attached to the safety harness correctly. My child seat had smashed into the back of the passenger side chair. I was a little small for the seat and the seat itself had taken the blow. No one was even sure if I'd been knocked out or asleep through the whole thing, but I was mostly unhurt. When I'd woken up, I'd walked away.

I don't remember anything about that. You'd think I would, considering I was found two miles from the accident along the side of the road, but nothing. They told me I was freezing cold, dirty and starving, and that it was a wonder I survived at all.

I slip the photo of my mom out from inside the folder, which I've read through a hundred times, and I look at her.

Did Vasily kill her? Why?

"Mommy, that's you!" Josh is suddenly beside me, wearing a circle of orange sauce around his mouth.

I tuck the photo away.

"That's actually your grandma," I tell him, putting the pen down and getting up. I've only written down that detail about the white streaks on the driver's side on the page. It's a sorry little list. "Let's get you cleaned up, and then we'll go for ice cream." I could use some fresh air too, honestly.

Once I have Josh bundled into a coat Talia had packed, I put my own on and take out my phone to text Lev and let him know what we're doing, but just as I start to type out my message, I get one from him.

Lev: On my way back. I'm about forty-five minutes away. Everything good there?

I consider my reply, knowing if I tell him I'm going to take Josh out for ice cream he'll tell me it's not safe and I should stay inside. But Josh is already pulling at my sleeve, and I can't take this away from him now. Besides, he's antsy and needs to burn off energy. Dairy Queen is literally around the corner, and I can't imagine Vasily's men would hang out there, so I type out a quick reply.

Me: Everything is fine. We'll see you soon.

"Put your hood up," I tell Josh as I do the same, checking to make sure I have cash in my purse, trying not to look at the pistol inside it.

I take his hand, and we step out into the cold night.

I'd never been to Providence before, and it's a cute town. I wish I could spend some time walking up and down Main Street, maybe doing a little shopping. The thought makes me long for the simplicity of a normal life.

Holding Josh's hand, we walk out of our room and down the empty hallway. Josh pushes the button for the elevator, and I watch the numbers on the screen as it climbs up to our room on the eighth floor.

Josh is excited about the elevator, and it's cute to see. Once we're inside, I show him which button to push, and we ride down in silence. One of the two desk clerks is busy checking in a guest while the other is on the phone. She looks up, and I smile as we walk outside.

The air is brisk but the night clear.

A man of about fifty stands outside the lobby doors smoking. He watches us as we pass, and I smile a hello, even as my heart races.

But I'm being paranoid. If Vasily's men were here, they wouldn't get a hotel room for the night. They'd get us.

"I see it!" Josh says, pointing at the brightly lit Dairy Queen when we turn the corner.

"What kind of sundae are you going to get?" I ask him even though I know. He always gets strawberry.

He considers this like he does every time I ask. "Probably strawberry."

From here, I can see that three tables are occupied with people eating their dinner or having ice cream. I find myself constantly looking around as we cross the two-lane road, and I push open the glass door.

Josh slips free of my hand and runs directly to the counter, face turned up to the menu with photos of the various creations, his hood sliding from his head.

I scan the restaurant, decide it's safe, and hurry to Josh.

"That one." He points at the strawberry sundae.

"That one it is," I tell him and order. Once I've paid, we wait a few minutes for the clerk to make the sundae. I plan on going back to the hotel room to eat it, but Josh insists on staying. He's bored. I get it. And I don't want him throwing a fit, so we take a seat in one of the booths.

My face is reflected back to me in the window that serves as a mirror with it being nighttime outside and so brightly lit inside. Looking at myself with dark hair triggers something. A memory.

I stare at my reflection for a long moment and remember one more detail about my mother.

She'd dyed her hair black too. And I know it's not my brain making up the memory because I remember waking up and being afraid when I didn't recognize her.

Had she done it to hide from Vasily or his men?

"Want a taste?" Josh asks me, calling me out of the memory. He's holding out a spoonful of ice cream with a smear of strawberry sauce.

"Please." I open my mouth and let him feed it to me. "Yummy!"

He smiles proudly and continues to eat.

I take out my phone to check the time, feeling anxious as new cars turn into the lot of the ice cream shop, although most use the drive-through window.

"You almost done?" I ask Josh who has slowed down about halfway in.

"The rest is for Wally." Which means he's full.

"Sounds good," I tell him, anxious to get out of here. I leave Josh in the booth as I walk to the counter to ask for a lid and a bag. The door opens, and in my periphery, I see two men enter the restaurant. The hairs on the back of my neck stand on end, and I can't help but turn to look at them.

As they walk toward the counter, I notice that one is looking in the direction of our booth where Josh is standing, trying to zip up his coat.

When I glance back at the man, he's watching me. I freeze, my heart in my throat.

"Cute kid," he says, then turns to the woman behind the counter, and they order two cones.

I hurry back to Josh and fumble to put the lid on the uneaten portion of ice cream, then help him zip up his coat. I don't bother with his hood as I walk us hurriedly out of the restaurant and back to the hotel.

"Slow down, Mommy."

I look down at Josh, who is struggling to keep up. "I'm sorry," I tell him.

A car honks its horn, startling me as it speeds past. I pull Josh backward, lifting him in my arms, dropping the rest of the ice cream.

"Mommy?" His tone is panicked, and when I

look at his face, his eyes are huge, and his lip is trembling.

"Shh, baby, it's okay. It's okay. Mommy needs to pay better attention, that's all. Let's go back and call Lev, okay? See how far he is."

He nods, and I keep him in my arms as I wait for another car to pass. As soon as I step out into the street, a big hand closes over my shoulder.

I gasp, spin to find one of the two men from the restaurant looming behind me. He tugs me backward as another car speeds past, catching me when I almost fall.

"I didn't mean to startle you," he says, letting me slip backward as I hug Josh who's watching the man too. "Here." He holds up Josh's scarf. "Found it in the booth when my friend and I sat down."

"My scarf!" Josh says, reaching out for it.

"Oh." I breathe a sigh of relief. "Thank you." I let Josh hold it.

"Are you okay?" the man asks me.

"Fine. We're fine. Thank you." I turn and hurry across the street back to the hotel on the verge of tears. I don't know if they're tears of relief or just from the stress of all of this, but I try to keep them hidden and am grateful it's dark as I try to get myself together before Josh sees me crying.

9

KAT

I decide not to mention our outing to Lev. I feel stupid for how I reacted to that man and also reckless for having gone out at all. There are men from the Russian mob looking for us, and it was just a stupid thing to do. I know Lev will be pissed, and I don't need that right now.

Josh is sleeping in the king-size bed of the studio-style hotel room. I'm sitting in the chair at the desk finishing the second little bottle of vodka while I watch him, his little face turned toward me, eyes closed, mouth slightly open as he hugs Wally to him, sleeping soundly.

After that night at Nina's, I didn't know what I'd do about the pregnancy. Abortion wasn't really ever an option for me. I understood that some women chose that route, but it just wasn't even something I considered. Maybe it was because of how I grew up, although the opposite makes more sense. But for me, I just knew how much I could love a child. Maybe it's that love I missed for all those years that did it. I wanted to have my own baby and give him all the love in the world like growing up showered with it is normal. Like it's the most normal thing in fact.

It should be.

Three quiet knocks sound on the door followed by a pause, then one more knock. Lev's signal.

When I get up to undo the chain—although I'm pretty sure that wouldn't keep anyone out who really wanted to get in—I breathe a sigh of relief to see Lev standing there in his signature leather jacket, hair flopping over his forehead, and his warm chocolate brown eyes smiling down at me.

I push into him, wrap my arms around his middle, and feel myself let go, at least a little. I inhale loudly, trying to stifle a sob.

He wraps his arms around me and walks me backward into the room.

"Hey." With a finger under my chin, he tilts my face up to his. "I'm sorry I'm so late." He pauses, studying me. "You okay?"

I nod. "I am now that you're here."

"Did something happen?" His expression changes. "Is Josh—"

"He's fine." I point toward the bed, and in the darkness, I know he can see Josh's little form under the blanket in the middle of the bed. "Sleeping."

"That's good." He closes the door and locks it, then takes my hand and looks me over again like he's making sure I'm okay.

"Why were you gone so long?"

He looks at the desk where the two empty little bottles of vodka sit. Going to the minibar, he opens it, then takes out another one of vodka and two of whiskey. He sits on the big armchair by the window and draws me down onto his lap.

Opening the vodka, he hands it to me.

I take it as he opens one of the whiskey bottles and drinks straight from it like I do mine.

"You already had a couple." He gestures to the empties on the desk. "That's not like you."

"I was worried. I *am* worried."

"I know. But it's going to be okay. We're going to get through this and have a life, Kat. You, me, and Josh."

"What kind of life? Running from hotel to hotel?"

He shakes his head, finishes the first bottle, and then opens the second. "No. I'll face Vasily head-on. He owes me some answers, and I owe him a bullet. And I won't tuck tail and hide. What we're doing now is to keep you and Josh safe and give me time to gather some ammunition. Get something on my uncle that'll end this."

"Like what?"

He finishes his second bottle. "I found the man I was looking for today."

"Who? I didn't know you were looking for someone."

"His name is Maxim Sobol. He used to work for Vasily."

"Lev, do you think that's safe or even smart?"

Josh mumbles something and rolls over to his other side. We've been talking in whispers, but I realize my whisper just got pretty loud.

"Relax, sweetheart." Lev tucks me against his chest and kisses the top of my head. "I think I may have something. In fact, you're going to meet him tomorrow."

WE LEAVE EARLY the next morning. I'm anxious as we head out, glancing at every closed door of the hotel, wondering who is inside, peering into each car in the parking lot, and still thinking about those men from last night when we pass the still-closed Dairy Queen. On the sidewalk, I see the bag I dropped that had the leftover ice cream. Josh is busy with one of the new toy trucks Lev bought him, and I'm grateful he doesn't mention our trip.

"So, you really think it was my mom on that list?" Lev's cousin had figured out that the name Kieran March on the list was actually my mother, Ciara March. March not being an uncommon name, I had paused when I'd seen it myself on the file, but not for long since Kieran is a man's name, and my mother had no connection to Vasily or anyone like him that I could imagine.

"Let's hear Maxim out. Let him tell it."

I meet his eyes. "So, we're about to meet a man who knew my mother."

Lev told me who Maxim was last night. Well, he gave me a brief history of his time together with him in Vasily's organization and told me that Vasily thinks Maxim is dead.

He also told me he'd been the hitman hired by Vasily to kill my mother.

"She'd dyed her hair like mine. I know that's a memory and not something I'm making up," I tell Lev again. "You really think she did it because she was running from Vasily?"

"Running from Vasily Stanislov or Gleb Mikhailov or maybe both."

"And Gleb is Vasily's boss."

"In a way, yes."

"I don't understand any of this." I slide down a little in my seat and look out the window.

"I have to go potty, Mommy," Josh's little voice says from the back seat.

I turn to look back at him. "You just went at the hotel, remember?"

"I have to go again."

I look at Lev. "There's an exit in about ten minutes. You think you can hold it until then, buddy?"

He nods and returns to playing with his truck.

"It's fine," Lev says. "I need to fill the tank anyway. Why are you so uneasy?"

"I think it's understandable, isn't it?"

He squeezes my knee, then keeps his hand there. "I promise nothing is going to happen to you or Josh."

"And what about you? What if something happens to you?"

He holds my gaze, then turns his out the window. "There's one more bit of news you should know."

"What?"

He glances in the rearview mirror, then turns to me. "Andrei isn't dead," he says quietly enough that Josh won't hear.

"What?" I feel the blood drain from my face.

"I'm pretty sure he's badly injured, and I'm going to take care of it, but I wanted you to know."

"How? And...oh my God. He's going to come after us too."

"Mommy?"

"Stay calm, Kat. It's going to be okay," Lev tells me. "Do it for Josh."

I press the heels of my hands into my eyes then turn to Josh.

"I really need to go."

"Almost there, baby."

Lev picks up speed, and we're turning off the exit not ten minutes later. He drives right up to the service area.

"I'll fill up the tank and come back for you. You stay inside until you see me."

I nod, climb out, then get Josh out. He's got Wally in one hand and the toy truck in the other.

"Should we leave those in the car?"

"No," he says and waves at Lev with the truck-hand.

I don't argue and walk in through the sliding glass doors and toward the ladies' room. The center is busy, and we have to wait in line for a few minutes, but pretty soon, it's our turn. When Josh is finished, I lift him up at the sink to wash his hands.

It's when we walk out that I see them.

Josh must see them at the same time because he stops, then waves. He recognizes the men from last night. They'd returned his scarf.

"Let's go," I tell Josh, pulling him along toward the door where, through the glass, I can see Lev at the pump across the parking lot.

"We'll use the other exit," the man says near enough to my ear to make me shudder. His hand falls on my shoulder again, like last night, except that today, it's heavier, and when I try to pull away, he shifts his grip to my upper arm, and I know he's not going to let go.

"You were getting ice cream," Josh says to the younger one, who is on Josh's other side and trying to take his hand.

"Let us go," I tell the bigger man at my side.

"My orders are to bring you and the boy in. That's all. I'm not going to hurt you, and you don't want to scare the kid, so act normal."

I look back over my shoulder and see the SUV still at the pump.

Shit.

"Please, I—"

"Wally!" I look down at the same moment Josh's hand slips from mine and see his other one in the younger man's hand as he separates us, walking him fast toward the exit at the back of the center. "I need Wally!" Josh is trying to get free of the man, body half-turned as he sees his stuffed animal farther and farther behind.

"I'll get you another toy," the man tells him in an

accented voice. If he'd spoken last night, I would have known. But the one who has me, he sounds American.

"He needs his toy!" I yell louder than I'm sure either of our companions like and loud enough that people stop and look.

"Fine," the one who has me says through gritted teeth. He leans toward me. "You grab it. We'll hold on to the kid for you."

I look at Josh as he's hurried out of the service area. I grab Wally and run after them, wondering how no one is stopping us. Don't they see what's happening?

We're out back in the next minute and headed toward a dark SUV with tinted windows. It's parked illegally, and the man who has Josh opens the back door as the older one grabs my arm again.

"Mommy!"

"I'm coming, Josh!" I run for him, but the one who has me won't let me get to him.

I remember the pistol still in my purse. It's loaded. Ready. But Josh is inside the SUV.

The younger man gets into the driver seat after closing Josh's door, and although I can't see him, I hear him calling for me as the older one walks me around to the other side.

Slipping my hand into my purse, I feel for the pistol. Just when I get my hand around the grip, I see the sliding doors open, and Lev rushes through them.

"Hey!" he calls out sharply, cocking the pistol he takes out from beneath his jacket. It's got a silencer on it. I can see that from here. "What you're taking doesn't belong to you." His voice is low, rage just beneath the surface of that false veneer of control.

"Motherfucker," the one who has me says and reaches beneath his jacket, eyes glued to Lev. That's when I pull my pistol out because he doesn't expect me to have one. He doesn't expect me to be armed or dangerous.

But I am.

I did it once before, but I was too late then. Joshua was already dead by the time I acted because I hesitated.

I won't be too late again.

And so, steeling myself, I cock my pistol, ram it under the fat belly of the man who has me, and in the same instant that he realizes what's happening, that he meets my eyes, I pull the trigger.

The pop is quieter than I expect. Maybe it's his fat that muffles the sound, I think, as the man stumbles backward, then slumps against the wall.

There's another sound, another popping. I open the back door to get Josh and can see Lev easing the younger man into the driver's seat.

Lev shifts his gaze behind me at the man now seated on the ground.

Josh stares up at me when I turn to him, dropping my pistol and grabbing him in my arms. I bury his face in my chest so he doesn't see the man on the ground.

"SUV is at the pump," Lev says to me. "Walk. Don't run."

I don't stop. Nodding, I walk fast through the service area, and I don't know if anyone notices us as we come out on the other side. I hurry across the lot to the pumps and to our SUV. I notice another one behind ours with its blacked-out windows. I see the bowed head of the driver, and I turn away.

Opening the back door, I situate Josh inside.

"Mommy?"

"Wasn't that funny to run into them again?" I ask him, my voice higher than usual and probably sounding like that of a crazed woman.

"What's happening?" He's confused.

Once he's strapped in, I hand him Wally, move my right hand up but stop and keep it out of sight when I spot the splatters of blood. I kiss the top of his head. I'm going to lose it in a second, so when Lev comes to take over, I let him.

"All set, kiddo?" he asks Josh, handing him a candy bar. "Hope you like Twix."

"Thank you," Josh says, still not quite sure what's going on.

Lev closes his door and turns to me. He looks me over, then nods. "Okay?"

I nod, although I'm nowhere near okay.

"You did good. We need to go. Now." He's all business and no emotion at all as he opens my door and lifts me in, strapping my belt in a matter of seconds before he's walking around the front of the SUV, in the driver's seat, and we're driving off, not speeding away, just heading toward the on-ramp to the highway. I glance at the back of the service center and see the parked SUV there.

"They were at Dairy Queen too," Josh says from the back seat as I hear the unwrapping of his candy bar.

"Were they?" Lev asks. "Didn't realize you'd gone to Dairy Queen without me," he adds on, eyes hard when they meet mine.

"We just—"

He closes his hand around my knee and squeezes, but this time, it's not just to reassure. "We'll discuss it later." He gestures to the glove compartment. "Clean up."

10

LEV

The drive to Maxim's house is quiet and filled with tension. Beside me, Kat stares out the window while Josh falls asleep in the back seat. We're going to have to talk about what happened today, but right now, all I can focus on is the fact that Vasily's men have already found us. The burning question in my mind is how.

More importantly, this means that there isn't a lot of time left for us in Providence. As soon as Vasily's men fail to check in with him, he'll know that we were here. But I can't leave without speaking to Maxim at least one more time. If he has information that might help us, I'm not going anywhere without it. I'm only hoping that he'll be more forthcoming once he meets Kat and Josh.

When we pull up to the driveway, Kat frowns at

the state of the place. She still isn't sure about this, but I'm hoping once she meets Maxim, she'll be more at ease too.

I shut off the car and remove Josh from the car seat, draping his sleeping body against my chest. Kat fidgets beside me as I ring the doorbell. The house is quiet inside, and the blinds move before Maxim comes to the door a minute later.

When he sees Kat standing there beside me, his eyebrows shoot up his forehead and he releases an audible gasp.

"Holy shit, kid." He shakes his head. "You weren't kidding. She looks exactly like her."

Kat offers him a nervous smile, and Maxim gestures us all inside.

"Have a seat." He points at the sofa. "It's not the Ritz, but I can offer you a glass of water if any of you are thirsty."

"We're okay," Kat answers. "But thank you."

Maxim nods, and for a moment, the two of them just study each other. Kat is the first to break the silence, reluctantly eager for information.

"Lev tells me you knew my mother?"

"I knew of her," Maxim says. "We weren't exactly friends. At least not at first anyway."

"What does that mean?" Kat squeezes my hand in hers, and I don't even think she realizes she's doing it.

Maxim looks at me, and I give him a subtle nod. I want Kat to know the truth. After today, she's proved that she's tougher than I ever wanted to believe. If she can handle Vasily's men coming at her, she can handle some hard realities too.

"I used to work for Vasily," Maxim explains. "That's the first I ever heard of your mother. She'd come into the club about once a week. It was always after we closed, but she'd sit at the bar and fidget with her keys. I always thought she looked out of place in that club. She was too pretty to be sitting there alone."

Kat swallows her emotion and smiles. "She was pretty."

"Well, if it's any consolation, you look just like her. In fact, if I didn't know better, I would have thought I'd seen a ghost on my doorstep this morning."

Kat nods, too choked up to speak.

"Anyway, I used to see her there every week. Vasily would come down and talk to her, and then she'd leave. It took me a while to figure out what was going on. It wasn't until I saw her at a Vory gathering on Gleb's arm that I started to piece shit together for myself."

"Gleb, the boss?" Kat looks at me.

"Yes." I nod.

"Vasily was using her. I don't know how she got

wrapped up with him in the first place, but I figured maybe he had something on her. That's how he got her to do his bidding."

"What do you mean?" Kat asks. "What was she doing?"

"She was running information about Gleb back to Vasily," I reply. "Vasily used her as a pawn. He wanted to take down Gleb."

"But things got complicated when your mother got pregnant," Maxim adds.

Kat's face pales, and she looks at me for confirmation of her silent thoughts. "Are you telling me that Gleb, the Russian mafia boss, is my father?"

"There's a strong possibility." I wrap my arm around her, brushing the hair off her shoulders as I do.

Kat seems to process that reality for a long time. "But why would she do that? Why would she help Vasily with anything?"

"She never told me." Maxim shrugs. "And I didn't ask. I figured that was her business, and in the end, she was so spooked, she wasn't going to tell anyone anything that wasn't necessary."

"Did she love Gleb?" Kat's voice fractures.

"It's hard to say." Maxim looks at me. "But if you're asking my two cents, I think she did. I think, in the end, it was really hard for her to know which way was up. By that point, it didn't matter what she did because the walls were closing in on her. If she came clean to Gleb, that was a big risk. And by turning her back on Vasily, she knew she was starting a war. But she did what she thought was best. For you."

Kat swipes away a few silent tears that have leaked from the edges of her eyes and shakes her head as she tries to process everything. It's a lot. But I know now that it was the right thing to do. She deserves to know her truth. Her backstory. Even if it's difficult.

"When I saw the name Kieran on the disk, I never even looked twice. I just assumed it was someone else."

"I think Vasily coded her that way in his own contacts," Maxim explains. "That way, if any of the Vory saw it, they wouldn't think anything of it either. He didn't want to take the chance of their connection getting back to Gleb."

"That makes sense," Kat murmurs. "I just... I still can't believe that he might be my father."

"Yeah." Maxim eyeballs me as he leans back into his recliner. "That could complicate things."

Kat looks at me. "How?"

"If Vasily makes this connection himself, then there's a chance he could try to use that against us. He could get to Gleb first. Spin this in another direction. I don't know."

"So we need to go to Gleb?" She twists her hands together in her lap.

"I need to go to Gleb," I clarify. "Test the waters. Then we can go from there. I'm not taking you anywhere near him until I have an idea how he's going to react to this news."

Maxim stands up and pads to the kitchen. "I think I have something that might help. At the very least, it couldn't hurt."

When he returns, he has a file in his hands. It looks like it's about a hundred years old. And I'm curious what it could be.

"Your mother's notes." He sets the file on the coffee table in front of us. "If you see Gleb, you can give these to him as proof that she didn't give Vasily everything. They are the original copies. The only copies."

"How did you get those?" Kat narrows her eyes at the yellow folder.

"Honestly?" Maxim sighs. "Vasily sent me after your mother. It wasn't something I was keen on doing, but you have to understand that in this line of work, you don't get much of a choice."

Horror washes over Kat's face as her gaze meets his. "Did you—?"

"No," he cuts her off. "The minute I saw she had a kid, I backed out. My loyalties to Vasily were already on thin ice at that point in my life, so I didn't want that on my conscience. I told your mother the truth. What I was sent there to do, and that I wouldn't be the only one. She understood that. But I suppose it was only a matter of time before it happened."

"Do you know who?" Kat presses. "Who killed her?"

Maxim looks at me, as if to say this is just another reason for me to go after the bastard. "It was Vasily. He did it himself."

Kat takes a deep breath and closes her eyes, shuddering. "I understand now. I get why he has to die. He's poison. Everything he touches, he destroys..."

Her words drift off right as Josh opens his eyes and stirs back to life, blinking sleepily as he glances around the unfamiliar surroundings.

"Hotel?" he murmurs.

"No, sweetheart." Kat leans over and kisses his forehead, stroking his hair back. "We are at a... friend's house."

Maxim gives Josh his best attempt at a non-threatening smile, but Josh just clings to my shirt, digging his fingers into the fabric so nobody can peel him away. It's second nature when I dip my head forward and kiss him on the top of his hair too. Kat watches the whole interaction, teary-eyed but happy. Despite all the shit happening around us, we still have each other. And I know now that she will fight for that.

The words are on the verge of spilling from my lips. Words I've never confessed to a woman other than my own mother. But I realize we still have an audience, and right now, I need to get us back on the road.

"We need to get going," I tell Maxim. "But there's something you should know."

"What is it?" he asks.

"There were a couple of men in the city already. They found us somehow. I took care of them, but—"

"The others won't be far behind," he finishes for me with a sigh. "I suspected as much."

"I didn't mean to bring trouble to your door." I meet his gaze. "But now that I have, I think it's best you leave too."

"Son of a bitch," Maxim grumbles under his breath. "I'm an old man now, kid. Life on the run is too hard for the likes of me."

"So maybe it's time to quit running," I say. "Come to New York. Help me with Gleb, and let's finish this once and for all. Together."

He leans back, glances around the shoddy house he calls home, and shrugs. "Ah, fuck it. What else have I got to do?"

"Where are we?" Kat stirs from her thoughts as we pull into the garage.

"It's a friend of Maxim's," I tell her. "We're going to trade vehicles again. I'll grab Josh."

She gets out of the car without a protest, resigned to the fact that this is our life for now. But I meant what I said. It won't always be that way. And I hope she can come to believe that at some point.

Maxim does the talking, and within twenty minutes, we have two different rigs to get back on the road. But before we leave Providence, there's just one more thing I need to do. We load up, and Maxim follows us to another service station just off the interstate.

"Stay here," I tell Kat. "I'll be right outside, okay?"

She nods, and I meet Maxim behind the SUV, pulling out the burner phone I took off Vasily's guys. Maxim's eyes collide with mine in quiet contemplation.

"I haven't trusted anyone in a long time, Lev."

"I know."

"Truth be told, I'm so goddamned paranoid, I'm still not even sure I can trust you. But you have a family in there, and I don't want to see the same thing happen to that girl that happened to her mother."

"I get it." I nod. "I don't want to see that either."

"I'm going to drip-feed you information," he says. "We'll take it one day at a time. For now, I think the thing you should start with is that neighbor who lived in your mother's building, Roger Benson."

"What about him?" I ask.

"He wasn't just the friendly neighborhood handyman. He was also a retired federal agent."

"Shit," I murmur. "That's who my mother was talking to?"

Maxim nods. "She probably thought he could help her. He probably thought he could too. Who knows? But the feds were hot on that case for a while, trying to figure out who did him in. Vasily was a paranoid fuck for months. He even went out of state for a while."

"I remember."

"You might want to lead with that. I'm going to go take a piss before we hit the road."

He walks off toward the service station, and I stare at the phone in my hand. There's no more putting it off. Vasily showed his hand today when he sent men after my family, again. And now, it's my turn to show mine.

I punch in the numbers, glancing at the SUV where Kat and Josh are securely tucked inside. The phone rings three times before Vasily picks up, half-breathless.

"Ivan," he grunts. "What the fuck—"

"I'm afraid Ivan can't come to the phone right now," I cut him off. "Or ever again, assuming that was the man you sent after my family today."

There is a moment of silence and then a low growl. "Levka."

"Hello, Uncle. I think perhaps it is time we discuss this business between us like men."

"Like men?" He snorts. "A man wouldn't run from his problems."

"A man wouldn't order the death of another man's woman behind his back," I return. "But I am coming to realize with each passing day that you were never a man at all. First my mother, your own blood, and now me? Is there anyone you will not betray to save your own skin?"

"Fuck you," he spits into the phone. "You shot Andrei. Your cousin. My son! Who the fuck do you think you are?"

My grip on the phone tightens as I lower my voice, so that he can be sure I'm in a rational mind. "I'm the man who's going to destroy you."

"I will send every soldier at my disposal after you. I will tear this country apart until your blood is spilled. And that of your son's—"

"You know, I am growing very tired of your empty threats." I meet Maxim's gaze as he returns to his car, nodding in my direction. "So, I think I will explain this in terms you can understand. Call off your fucking dogs now, or I will have no choice but to unleash every one of your dirty secrets for the entire world to see."

"Secrets." He laughs darkly. "You have nothing on me."

"Oh, but I do. That drive you were so intent on finding? I have that list of names. And it's funny what connections you can make from such a simple document. Like the fact that the neighbor you murdered in my mother's building was a retired fed."

Silence is the only response on the other end of the line, and if it wasn't for his heavy breathing, I wouldn't even be sure he was still there. But I've got his attention now. And I'm going to run with it.

"There is also the cop that you killed," I continue. "My mother. Nina's father. After all, it's his name on your list. How many others? Too many connections to count. Deaths that can all be linked back to you."

"You wouldn't fucking rat on your family," he snarls. "You may be a lot of things, Lev, but a snitch isn't one of them."

"I'll do whatever it takes to secure my future," I assure him. "Even if that means throwing you to the wolves."

"I think you're forgetting something." His voice changes to one of amusement. "Betray the Vory, and you will bring down a whole world of pain on yourself. So, go ahead, talk to the feds. See what happens."

"Ahh... but that's the thing. I'm not betraying the Vory, am I? I'm only betraying you. Who sanctioned all these hits? I don't think I need to tell you that the chain of command was broken in every instance."

"And I think you're forgetting something," Vasily replies. "A Vor will always back another Vor. You were never inducted. If it comes down to you or me, it will always be me."

"We'll see."

On the other end of the line, I can hear him twisting the seal of his beloved vodka. He won't admit that I have him at a disadvantage. I already knew he wouldn't back down. Even if it costs him his freedom, he will never let a slight go unpunished.

"You think you are so smart," he says finally. "Calling me to threaten me like a little bitch. But there is a complication that you did not foresee. Something even I did not see. Perhaps you care to venture a guess?"

In the pit of my stomach, I know what he's referring to. But he's testing me. He wants to know if I know about Kat's relation to Gleb, which means that he's made the connection himself. It's the only thing he could be referring to.

"Maybe I won't kill your little bitch when I find her," he says, answering my unspoken thoughts.

"She might come to be useful after all. You, however, I can't say the same for."

"So, this is how you choose to proceed?" My hand balls into a fist.

"Come at me with everything you've got, Lev," he answers darkly. "Because I won't rest until I've hunted you like a dog and destroyed everything you love. Mark my words."

11

KAT

I sit amid bubbles in a tub big enough for two at what is probably one of the nicest places I've ever stayed in. I thought Lev would choose a quiet hotel out of the way, but we're at a high rise in Times Square in the heart of everything.

Even though I grew up in Philadelphia, I've never been to New York City. Josh has his face plastered to the floor-to-ceiling glass wall, Wally in one hand, little toes peeking out from beneath his new Minion pajamas and staring in awe at everything. He didn't even fight me when it came time to take his bath when he saw the size of the tub. I guess to him it was like a small swimming pool. Which there is an indoor one here and Lev has promised to take him swimming tomorrow.

"Time for bed, Josh," Lev says from the doorway

of the bathroom. It's so big, I'm pretty sure the entire cabin Josh and I rented in Colorado could fit inside it.

When Josh doesn't reply, Lev goes to him and crouches down beside him. He wraps one arm around Josh's shoulders to point out something, and I think about how right this is. How right that he's with us. Even with everything going on, I don't have to do it alone, and I didn't realize how much of a weight that's been all these years.

Josh giggles as Lev makes a joke, then lifts him up in his arms and walks him toward me.

"Night, Mommy," Josh says, rubbing his eyes.

Lev leans him down, and I plant a kiss on the top of his head.

"Night, baby," I say and watch them walk out through our bedroom and to the connecting one. A few minutes later, I hear the familiar words of *Good Night, Gorilla*. I lean my head back against the cool ceramic of the tub and close my eyes.

My mom was somehow involved in this world. How? And who would know? Vasily, but he would just as soon kill me than tell me anything. My father?

My father.

My mom was in love with him, according to Maxim.

I sit up, disturbing the bubbles.

My mother was in love with a mobster. Not only that, but the boss of them all. And she ran information on him to Vasily? That doesn't make sense. Why would she do that? Is Maxim right that he was blackmailing her? Or that Vasily "had something on her," as he put it?

She was barely twenty when she gave birth to me. How much could there be to "have" on a person?

"He's out cold," Lev says not ten minutes later, leaning against the doorframe with arms folded across his chest.

"He must be exhausted with everything that's happening."

He nods. "You didn't kill him, by the way."

"What?"

"We didn't get a chance to talk about it, but if you're feeling guilty or upset about the guy at the service station, your bullet didn't kill him. Mine did."

Is there something wrong with me that I didn't care about that man? Should I feel guilty?

"I don't," I tell Lev.

He studies me in that way of his that he's always had. Like he can see right into my mind.

I stand and watch him sweep his gaze over me as soapy water glides off my body.

"I don't feel guilty or upset or anything, Lev. Maybe you should know that about me." I step onto the mat, and I feel his eyes on me when I walk across the room to the stand-up shower and reach in to switch it on.

I hear the click of the door closing and the lock engaging when I step beneath the flow of steaming water to rinse off.

A minute later, he's naked and in the shower with me, hands around my waist, turning me to face him.

"What do you think I should know about you that I don't already?" His gaze locks on mine as one hand slides between my legs.

"That's two men I've killed," I say.

"I just told you, you didn't kill him."

"I wanted to. And he would have bled out if you'd left him."

"But he didn't."

I stare up at him, and I don't know why I feel defensive and angry. No, I do. Because a part of me blames him even though I know Josh and I were never really safe out in Colorado. I knew this was always going to chase us.

"What is it?" he asks.

"Just let me go." I push his hand off me. "I'm tired."

"I'll never let you go. Don't you know that yet?"

He grips a handful of hair, hauls me up to my tiptoes and kisses me, his other hand cupping my ass, his cock like a steel bar between us.

"You're mine, Katya. You belong to me. Forever. I will take care of you. There's nothing you can say or do that will make me let you go." He takes my earlobe between his teeth and bites, sending electricity to my core.

"I'm tired." I push against him but trying to move him is like trying to move a brick wall.

"You need to come."

"Let go."

"No." He tugs my head backward. "I should punish you, you know," he says.

He presses my back to the wall, and his fingers dig painfully into the skin of my inner thigh as he lifts one leg. He bends his knees a little, eyes locked on mine. My arms wrap around his neck as he lifts me and thrusts into me hard.

I gasp, taking his full length, the stretch painfully good and the sensation of him inside me like this, filling me up like this, I want it.

No, it's more than want. I need it.

"Does your silence tell me that yes, I should punish you?" He thrusts, and I let out a grunt.

"He was bored. He wanted ice cream," I say.

"And he can have ice cream. If you'd told me about those men, I wouldn't have left you alone at the service center. I wouldn't have let you out of my sight, and what happened wouldn't have happened."

"What if the worst would have happened? What

if they'd taken him? What if they'd..." I can't finish, and he doesn't want me to.

Lev pulls out of me, takes my face in both hands, and brings his forehead to mine.

"Let it go. It's over, and we're all fine."

"Fine?"

"Fine."

"How can you say that?" I start, but he doesn't reply. Instead, he switches off the shower. Lifting me, he hoists me over his shoulder, smacks my ass once, and carries me into the bedroom. He tosses me onto the bed and closes the connecting door between our room and Josh's.

"What are you doing? Leave that open."

"I don't think you want him to hear me fucking you, and you do need to be fucked, Kat."

"Lev—"

He grabs my ankle, pulls me flat on the bed, then flips me onto my stomach. He slaps my ass again.

"Lev!"

"Don't worry, you're safe," he says, gripping my cheeks and spreading me open. "At least from my hand."

He thrusts into me, and I arch my back to take him as he fists my hair again, tugging my head backward and stilling deep inside me.

"From now on, you tell me everything, Kat. Every little inconsequential detail. You got that?"

I wriggle my hips beneath him, wanting him to move, and when he won't, I slide my hand between my legs.

Chuckling, he takes my wrist and draws my hand away.

"That pussy's mine, too, sweetheart. You don't touch it without my permission anymore." He stretches that arm and my other over my head and closes both hands over a rung of the metal headboard. "Keep them there."

He thrusts once more, then draws out of me. His breath is warm against my cheek as I feel his hand slide between my cheeks, rub against my pussy, then find my other hole.

"What are you doing?" I start, trying to pull away.

He doesn't let me, though. Just starts moving his fingers back and forth, and back and forth, smearing my own arousal into me.

I still, too embarrassed but also aroused.

"This is mine too, this tight little hole."

When he pushes his finger inside me, I tighten all my muscles.

"You can't...you're too big!"

He turns my head, so I have to look at him from the corner of one eye.

"You're right, it's going to be a tight squeeze," he says, moving his finger in and out, and in and out. "But we'll make it work."

He pulls his finger out and slides himself between my ass cheeks, rubbing his length against my ass before bringing the head of his cock to my entrance and gently pushing against me.

"Lev." It's a whimper as he takes my clit between his fingers.

"You need to be fucked. You'll feel better after you're fucked. Isn't that right?"

I nod because this feels too good.

"Then answer my question. Tell me you understand that you will tell me every single thing so I can fuck your tight little ass already."

"Yes. Yes. I understand." I nod my head, arching my back, and when he lets me, I shift to my knees, and he settles between them.

"You're perfect, you know that?" he asks, fingers still working my clit as he takes inch by slow inch of me. "Perfect for me."

I come then, with him moving inside me and his fingers rubbing my clit. I bury my face in a pillow, and that's when he pushes all the way into me and begins to fuck me. To really fuck me.

I tumble from one orgasm to the next, lost, my mind a fog, and when I feel him throb inside me, when I feel him empty, I come again, one final time as he lays his full weight on me like he's empty too, like he's given everything to me.

12

KAT

Lev cleans me gently afterward, dresses me in one of his T-shirts, and tucks me into the crook of his arm on the bed.

He was right. I did need to be fucked. I feel better. Lighter.

I glance at the door between our rooms, which Lev opened again. If I listen closely, I can hear Josh's even breathing.

"Why didn't Maxim stay here too?" I ask. The older man said he'd see us tomorrow and disappeared before we got to the hotel.

"He's been in hiding a long time. He wants to trust me, and he wants to help you and Josh, but Vasily would kill him if he knew he was alive. I'd do the same if I were in his shoes."

I nod. Makes sense. "The man at the service

station, he said something I didn't really think about then."

"What was it?"

"He said that his order was to take me and 'the kid'. He said he didn't want to hurt us."

"Vasily knows, Kat. He knows who you are."

"Which means he won't want to kill Josh or me? Even though he killed my mom?"

"He's a sick bastard. I don't think he'd let you live out of any kindness, and as long as Gleb doesn't know you exist, all bets are off. But if Gleb found out..."

"But that could lead to a whole other scenario and possibly not a good one."

"I think he'd want to protect you and Josh. It's just my gut feeling."

"What if he doesn't believe it?"

"After seeing you, he'll at least be willing to listen. You look exactly like her. He could run a paternity test if he wanted to. And either way, he has no reason to want you or Josh hurt."

"I've seen what's on that drive."

"And I wonder what he'll make of it when he sees it."

"What if he does accept that I'm his daughter and that he should protect us but then wants us to be a part of that life? Wants Josh to be a part of it?"

"You'll drive yourself insane going in circles like this. We have to wait and see."

"And what about you? Will he protect you from Vasily?"

"Don't worry about me. I can take care of myself."

He brushes a strand of damp black hair off my face. "I want my hair back. I want to keep looking like her. It's the only piece of her I have."

"Soon. I promise."

"Do you think it's true? That Vasily killed her himself?"

"I don't know, Kat. But Maxim has no reason to lie."

"He tried to help her. At least she had one friend in the end." I look up at him and realize how selfish I'm being. He lost his mom too and to the same murderer. "Tell me about your mom."

He takes a deep breath in, and his eyes alight on the small jewelry box that I set on the table when fishing for Josh's pajamas.

"She was kind and gentle. She never wanted anything from my uncle. And when I think back now, I see things differently. I see how she tried to shield me from him. See how she was when she was around him, jittery and skittish. I think she was always afraid of her own brother. Maybe she knew what he was capable of all along even when it came to his own blood."

His expression changes, growing darker.

"I need to do something. Stay here."

I clutch his arm. "Don't leave, Lev. Please, just tonight. I need you to stay."

He leans down, cups my cheek, and kisses my forehead. "I'm not going anywhere, Katya." He gets up off the bed. I watch him walk across the room, the muscles on his bare back working, making my stomach flutter.

"What are you doing?" I ask, sitting up to watch him dig his phone out of his jeans pocket.

"William von Brandt had a contact at the FBI." He sits on the edge of the sofa, pushes a few buttons, and holds the phone out in front of him.

"Lyoshenka." I recognize Alexei's voice.

"Alexei," he says. "Sorry to call so late."

I'm surprised he doesn't switch to Russian.

"It's all right. I would have called you tomorrow anyway."

"You have the information then? William von Brandt's contact at the FBI, did you find his name?"

"Of course. It took a little work, but I enjoyed the challenge. But Lev, I'm concerned—"

"Send it all to me. Everything."

"What are you going to do with it?"

"I think you know."

Alexei draws a sharp breath in. "You know what that will make you?"

"Yeah, I know."

"It won't be only Vasily coming after you."

"I'm willing to take that risk."

"What?" I ask, every hair on my body standing on end.

"I have to do this, Alexei. It's him or me, and even if it weren't, I owe him for my mother's murder at the very least."

"I advise against this."

"I'll keep you out of it. You and your family won't be linked to this."

I can almost hear Alexei's disapproval in his silence. "You'll have it in a few minutes."

"Thank you, cousin."

He disconnects the call, then walks to the bed to sit on the edge of it as he dials another number. When I open my mouth to speak, he puts a finger to his lips, and I hear a woman click on.

"Philadelphia Police Department."

"You have a pen and paper?"

"What?"

"A woman went missing from Club Delirium a few nights back. You'll find her body at a house owned by Andrei Stanislov. He just planted a new garden." After rattling off an address, he disconnects the call, takes a deep breath in, then lets it out, and sets the phone on the nightstand.

"What did you just do?"

He turns to me, closing his big hand over my knee. "I'm just keeping Vasily busy for a day or two. I need time. Get some sleep. I have to make a few more calls."

"What calls? Why did Alexei say they'd all come after you? Does that mean not just Vasily?"

He gets up and goes to where the duffel bag is. He digs through it to take out the folder that contains the information on my mother as well as a print-out of what was on that drive.

"What do you have to do, Lev?"

A ding signals an email on his phone. He shifts his attention to it, punches something in, then puts his phone down and looks at me.

"I'm going to turn over evidence to William von Brandt's contact at the FBI."

13

LEV

Josh finishes up his eggs and rubs his belly before he slips away from the table. Kat and I both watch him as he toddles over to me, Wally dangling from one hand while he studies the spread of documents I've been stuffing into the manila envelope.

"What are you doing?" he asks curiously.

"I have to send out a package." My eyes meet Kat's across the room, and she can't hide her nerves.

We both know this is a last-resort option. I don't need to tell her that I'm doing this just in case I don't come back today.

"Can I help?" Josh asks.

"I'll tell you what, buddy." I scoop him up and set him on the bed beside me. "Why don't you wait here for a second? I have the perfect job for you. But it's top secret, okay? Just between us guys. Can you handle that?"

He giggles and eyeballs his mom, who is suddenly pretending not to hear. When I walk over and grab my mother's trinket box from the nightstand, I sneak a glance at Kat as she disappears into the bathroom to wash up. She knows we're up to no good, but she's just as much a silent participant in these shenanigans.

I kneel in front of Josh and open the box, and his eyes go wide as he studies the jewelry inside.

"What do you think your mom would like?" I ask him. "Can you help me pick something out?"

He nods eagerly, his stubby fingers pulling out a bracelet and then a ring to examine them. It's hard not to get choked up when I see that ring. It was the same piece my father gave to my mother many years ago as a symbol of their love. A vintage blue sapphire ring from the 1920s that still sparkles like the day he gave it to her, or at least, that's what I'd like to believe.

"Blue," Josh says. "I think Mommy will like this one."

A grin tugs at my lips as I lean closer and give him a conspiratorial whisper. "I think you're right, buddy."

He hands the ring over to me, and I stuff it into my pocket with a wink just as Kat reappears with a hairbrush in her hand. She eyes us both cautiously and then comes to sit on the other side of Josh.

"Should I even ask what you boys are up to?"

Josh shakes his head, his expression dead serious. "No. Top secret."

"That's right." I ruffle the hair on his head with a smile. "Bro code."

Kat rolls her eyes and then glances at the box in Josh's lap. "Is that your mother's?"

"Yes."

"I thought so," she says softly.

Josh pulls out the locket and pries it open with his fingers, squinting to examine the small photo.

"Mommy, look it's me." Josh points at the boy in the photo, and we both laugh.

"No, honey, that's Lev."

"Lev?" Josh's brows scrunch together as he studies the photo beside it. The one with my mother and father too.

"Do you have a daddy, Lev?" When he looks at me, it's the most innocent of questions, but it hits me like a fucking missile to the chest. "Because I don't have a daddy."

Something squeezes my hand, and when I look down, I realize it's Kat. When our eyes collide, there's a softness in hers as she nods her approval. This is the moment I've been waiting for. The moment that changes everything.

"Actually, sweetheart." Kat kneels before him to meet him at eye level. "That's something we want to talk to you about. Do you remember when I told you that some boys have daddies at home and some don't?"

"Yes." Josh nods.

"Well." She swallows and looks up at me. "You do have a daddy. Lev is your daddy."

For a full minute, it feels like I could hear a pin dropping while I wait for Josh to say something. And when he turns to me, his face lit with happiness, he surprises us both when he sets down the box and crawls into my lap to give me a hug.

"I like Lev," he says. "Lev is my daddy."

It's such a simple thing, but it feels like the proudest moment of my life as I hug him back, my throat almost too hoarse to speak.

"That's right, buddy," I tell him. "I'm your father, and we're a family now."

Then, a little quieter, I lean into his ear, whispering my truth as Kat chokes up beside me. "I love you, Josh. Always."

"Why do I get the feeling this is way scarier than you're making it out to be?" Kat asks.

"It's not," I lie, reaching down to stroke her hair

one more time. "I'll be back this evening, sweetheart."

She doesn't look convinced, and she shouldn't be.

"But just in case—"

"Here it comes." Tears spring to her eyes, and she shakes her head. "I don't want to hear just in case."

"It's just a safety measure," I tell her. "You know this, baby."

She wraps her arms around herself, trying to pull it together, and it only makes me realize how far we've come. She's terrified to lose me, and it isn't just because she's afraid. This is so much more, and I'm tempted to get down on one knee right now and claim her as mine, but I don't want it to be under these circumstances.

"If I'm not back tonight by eight, remember what I told you."

"Call Alexei." She nods stiffly.

"And take the cash out of the safe. Take everything with you. This will all be over soon, but in the meantime, you can trust him, Kat."

"Don't make me trust him." She clutches at the collar of my jacket. "Just come back to us."

"I will." My lips graze hers one last time, and I pull the ring from my pocket. "I have something for you."

When she notices the ring in my hand, she sucks

in a breath before her gaze collides with mine. "Lev?"

"I just want you to wear it for now." I take her hand in mine and slip it onto her right ring finger. "It was my mother's, and I want you to have it. But more importantly, I want you to think about me every time you look at it."

"Ha, ha." She slaps my chest and then gives me a watery smile. "It's beautiful. I'll never take it off."

"You will," I promise her, "when we make it official. But for now, just remember that even if it doesn't always feel like it, I'm doing all of this for you."

"I know," she murmurs.

"Kat?" I clutch her face in my hands, forcing her gaze to mine. "I fucking love you, sweetheart. I want you to know that."

14

LEV

Downstairs, I slip the manila envelope to the concierge with a crisp hundred-dollar bill on top.

"I need this to go out tomorrow morning," I tell him. "Not today. Not tomorrow afternoon. Tomorrow morning only. Can you make that happen?"

"Yes, of course." He nods. "Anything you want, sir."

"How long is your shift today?" I ask him.

"I'll be here until nine, sir."

"Good." I slip him another hundred. "If I come back for it, you give it to me. But if I don't, nobody else gets it, no matter who they are. You just send it off tomorrow morning. We clear?"

"Clear." He dips his head. "I will handle it personally for you, sir."

"Very good."

I leave him with the package and make my way toward the exit, but before I get there, my phone rings. When I see it's Alexei, I dart into a corridor and answer.

"Lyoshenka," I greet him. "To what do I owe the pleasure?"

"You're in a good mood today." He quirks an eyebrow at me. "For a man who might not live to see the day through."

"You know how it is." I shrug. "We've got to make the best of it."

"Ah yes, well..." He scratches at his chin. "I have some news."

"What is it?"

"The cops raided Andrei's house. Dug up the backyard. Couldn't find anything. The place was spotless."

"Son of a bitch," I growl. I knew that was a fucking trap. Vasily probably had the body out of there the next day.

"However"—Alexei holds up a finger—"it appears they did find some CCTV footage of Andrei with the missing girl that night. A clerk at a gas station called in the tip."

"Well, that's something," I murmur, "but not exactly what I was hoping for."

"It's enough to create a distraction," Alexei says. "Andrei is still in the hospital, but my sources tell me they've questioned him twice already. Vasily has disappeared, gone into hiding by all accounts, but I suspect he's on his way to New York."

"I suspected as much myself." I nod. "We don't have much time."

"No, you don't," Alexei agrees.

"If you are giving free bad advice, I'm in the market." I tease him with a smile.

"Lead with Ciara." Alexei grins back at me. "Always lead with the woman."

"Are you ready for this?" I ask.

Maxim looks at me like I'm fucking delusional. "Ready to go get my nuts blown off? Yeah sure, kid. Every day of the week and twice on Sundays."

Despite the gravity of the situation, I laugh. Being around the old man again makes me remember why I liked him so much to begin with.

"Well, at least you can take comfort in the fact that you're so fucking old you probably don't even need your nuts anymore," I tell him. "I have a woman back at the hotel who's grown rather fond of mine. So, let's try to keep them in one piece, yeah?"

He shrugs and eyeballs the club. "You sure this is even the right place?"

"Yes. I have good intel that he comes here every Wednesday like clockwork."

"Well, even a good clock can be wrong." Maxim shrugs.

We wait in silence, scoping out the building. It's more upscale than Delirium, but I don't know the layout. I don't know anything about what awaits us inside, or what's going to happen when Gleb actually shows up. He has a reputation for being ruthless, but I suspect at least half of that is just Vory folklore, and the rest is probably the truth.

It takes two full hours before I finally catch a glimpse of him. A black SUV pulls up to the curb, idling while one of his soldiers comes around to the back and opens the door for him. When the old man steps out, he glances down both sides of the street even though his soldiers have already checked twice. A force of habit, I suppose. When you're the man at the top of the food chain, there is no shortage of men who'd like to take your place.

Maxim and I don't even speak as we approach, and we don't manage to get within ten feet of him before one of his soldiers reaches for his weapon.

"Who the fuck are you?" Gleb turns to me, eyes dark and hard.

I have a feeling we're both about to get shot the fuck up, but before he gives the order, his eyes move to Maxim, and recognition sparks.

"Hold up," he tells his men. "I know this one. Aren't you supposed to be dead?"

"Something like that." A smile curves Maxim's lips. "But I've got a few more lives left in me yet."

"Maxim," Gleb says his name. "You worked for Vasily back in the day, right?"

"The one and only." Maxim nods.

"What business do you two have here?" Gleb asks, his eyes darting to me. "And who the fuck are you?"

"I'm Vasily's nephew," I answer carefully, hoping that Vasily hasn't spoken with him yet. "Lev."

"We were hoping to have a private audience with you," Maxim says. "Just a few minutes of your time."

One of his soldiers steps forward, glaring in our direction. "Boss, I don't know if that's such a good—"

Gleb holds up his hand, silencing him immediately. "What's this about?"

There are a lot of ways I could spin this, but all I can think about is what Alexei said, and I know he's right.

"It's about Ciara March."

For a split second, the hardness in Gleb's eyes

vanishes, washing away beneath a tidal wave of pain as he repeats her name. "Ciara?"

I nod. Maxim shifts beside me. We wait in tense silence, uncertain how he's going to react. Even after all these years, it's obvious she still affects him. The mere mention of her name opened a raw wound, and for all I know, it could be something he wants to forget.

"Pat them down and take them inside." Gleb gestures to his men. "Make it quick."

He leaves us on the sidewalk while his men disarm us and take our phones while they're at it too. Once they are satisfied that we aren't wearing a wire, they lead us inside, through the club, and down to the basement.

Maxim glances at me in question, and I just shrug. Either we're walking to our deaths right now, or this is where Gleb conducts his business.

When we get to the bottom of the stairs, Gleb is waiting at a bar that appears to be set up for his own private use. He gestures for us to sit down beside him, and then looks at his men.

"Put in some headphones. We're going to have a conversation."

The soldiers do as he requests. Standing like sentinels at the entrance to the stairs, they watch us carefully as Gleb pours three glasses of vodka.

"It's been a long time since I've heard her name."

He slides a glass in my direction, following up with one for Maxim. "How did you know her?"

Maxim looks at me, and I nod at him to go ahead.

"Ciara used to come into the club," he tells Gleb. "In Philly."

Gleb stares at him like he's reaching into his soul, and already, I can see the tension creeping in around his eyes. We need to tread carefully here, and I just hope Maxim chooses his words with caution.

"Once a week, she'd meet with Vasily. I never spoke with her at that time and didn't know much about her. But I started to piece together what I suspected their business was after I saw her at a Vory gathering with you."

"Go on," Gleb orders.

"Then one day, out of the blue, Vasily tells me I need to take care of her. That she's a problem. So that's exactly what I went to do."

Gleb's fingers tighten around his glass, and I feel my own muscles responding in kind as Maxim rushes to get the rest out.

"But then I saw her, and I couldn't do it. No fucking way. I didn't like to run jobs on women, and excuse me for what I'm about to say, but I was tired of Vasily's shit. Every other week, someone new was marked for death."

"What happened to her?" Gleb growls.

"I spoke to her," Maxim says. "Told her to get the fuck out of town. I explained to her that I wouldn't be the only one Vasily would send. She understood that. And that's when she gave me these."

Maxim retrieves the photocopies of the notes he took last night, pulling them from his jacket and setting them onto the bar in front of Gleb. For a minute, Gleb just stares at them, thumbing through them before he closes his eyes, revealing an obvious shudder when he speaks.

"She betrayed me."

"At first," Maxim concedes. "That was her intention. But I think what you had with her was real. In the end, she didn't want to hurt you anymore. She felt trapped, and she was too afraid to come to you and too afraid to stay. So, she gave me these and told me to keep them safe. That maybe one day, you could understand."

"I always understood." Gleb sighs. "I suspected she was running information back to someone in the Vory, I just didn't know who. When I confronted her with it, she denied it. I went out to do a job that day, and when I got back, she was gone. I never saw her again, but I've been looking all these years."

"I'm sorry to tell you that Vasily got to her," Maxim says. "Just a couple of years after she took off."

Gleb hangs his head, and even from where I'm

sitting, I can feel the pain radiating from him. It's obvious that despite what Ciara did, what they had was real, and Gleb has never gotten over it.

"Vasily did this?" he asks, with a haunting finality.

"Yes," I answer.

He tilts his head up to meet my gaze. "And what does any of this have to do with you? Why would you betray your uncle to come here with this information? You aren't even inducted. You owe me nothing."

He's suspicious of me, and I can't say that I blame him. But I lay it all out for him.

"I have a few reasons to care," I say. "The first being that he murdered my mother, and I suspect my father too. The police said he was mugged, but it just seems too coincidental."

"And the third reason?" Gleb presses.

I look at Maxim, my chest constricting as I make the biggest gamble I've ever made in my life. "They are twofold actually. And I hope you can understand why I'm hesitant to tell you. But what you felt for Ciara? I feel that way about her daughter."

"Daughter?" Gleb's eyes shoot up, bouncing between Maxim and me. "What... *daughter*?"

"I suspect that would be your daughter," Maxim answers. "Or at least, that's what I concluded when I saw her with the baby after she ran out on you."

The room falls silent for a long moment, and I know there's nothing else I can say right now. Gleb is digesting the information, turning it over in his mind, trying to make heads or tails of it. It's a situation I can relate to well, considering my own circumstances when I found Kat.

"I find it difficult to believe," he says finally.

"I thought you might." I remove the fake driver's license Kat used in Colorado, sliding it across the bar toward him. "But genes don't lie."

His finger moves over her face, examining her, and he shakes his head, his voice fracturing when he speaks. "It's like seeing a ghost."

"I can bring her to meet you," I tell him. "If that's what you want. I think she has a few things she'd like to tell you herself."

He downs the glass of vodka in front of him and stares at the wall ahead to hide his emotion. "I would like that very much."

"I need your assurances that she will be safe," I tell him. "I intend to make her my wife. And I'm not letting her go."

Gleb glances at me, and the smallest glimpse of respect flashes in his eyes. He's not used to anyone speaking to him this way. He gives the orders. He tells other people how things will go. But when it comes to Kat, I'm not willing to concede on this.

"She will be safe," he answers. "And the other part, well time will tell if you are worthy."

A grin tugs at my lips, and I nod. "There's just one more thing we need to discuss."

"Ah, yes." He reaches for the bottle of vodka in front of him and pours another glass. "Vasily."

15

KAT

"Can we swim now, Mommy?"

I turn from the window to find Josh has stripped down to his underwear and is clutching Wally. He's standing by the door with his hand on the doorknob, and I remember Lev had promised to take him swimming today.

I have to smile when I walk toward him and crouch down so we're at eye level. I brush hair back from his face and think how much like Lev's it is. How it constantly flops this way or that no matter what I do with it.

"Why are you in your underwear, Josh? Where are your clothes?"

"Daddy said he'll take me swimming."

Daddy. How easily he accepts this. It's a relief.

"Ah," I say. "I guess in lieu of a swimsuit, you thought your briefs would do. Smart."

I ruffle his hair and check the time. Late morning. The minutes are crawling by as I wait for Lev to return, fighting back that niggling thought that he might not return.

"I'll tell you what, let's get you dressed because you can't swim in your undies and Mommy certainly can't either, so we'll go down to the gift shop and buy new swimsuits. Would you like that?"

He nods enthusiastically, and I go to retrieve his clothes from the floor of his bedroom. Once he's dressed, I type out a quick text to Lev.

Me: I'm taking Josh swimming. Don't worry, we'll be safe.

I wait, hoping for a response or even acknowledgment that he's read the text, but I get neither.

"Mommy." Josh tries the door handle, but it won't open because of the extra lock.

"All right, all right," I say, dropping our room key into my purse where the gun I used the other day is. I guess Lev put it back when I didn't know.

My belly feels tense. I hate this. I hate all of this.

Taking Josh's hand, I open the door and set the Do Not Disturb sign on the outside of it. I smile at the two housekeepers chatting in the hall as we make our way to the elevator. We're alone as we ride down to the lobby.

The hotel is busy. There are a restaurant and bar, which I'm sure draws in tourists and guests alike. The energy in the air is one of excitement and fun, but I'm on the outside of that.

Scanning the lobby, I don't see anyone out of the ordinary, and no one even glances up as we walk through to the gift shop.

I must not be moving fast enough because Josh tugs at my hand and points at the little store. We walk in, and Josh goes directly to the area with floats and pool toys. I follow him and find the rack of swimsuits for kids. The price tags give me pause, but it's this or our underwear, and I don't really want to get kicked out of the pool, so I hold up two suits in his size.

"Minions or Marvel?"

"Minions!"

"Minions it is."

"Mommy?" Josh holds up a pair of floaties with —surprise—minions on them and a ball.

"All right. Why not? Come on, Mommy needs a suit too. I can't swim in my underwear, can I?"

"No. Silly Mommy."

I buy the least expensive suit I can find, which still gives me sticker shock at eighty dollars. I hate that Lev will have to pay for these things because I have about twenty-five dollars on me, but I charge it all to our room and ask the girl to cut off the tags before we leave.

Josh happily carries his ball, and I take our bag to head to the pool, which is one floor down. I can already smell the chlorine as the elevator descends, and when the doors open, I find a large indoor pool busy with families with children ranging from babies to pre-teens.

Josh is so excited that he puts down his ball and starts to strip right there.

"Whoa, kiddo," I tell him, and I have to laugh. "Changing rooms are right there."

"Okay." He picks up his ball again, and we go into the changing rooms to put on our suits. I decide to keep the rest of our things in a locker, including the gun in my purse, because with all these families around, there's no way I'd use it.

Grabbing two towels and Josh's floats, we head to the pool, and I take a seat to blow up the floats. Once they're secured around Josh's arms, he runs and fearlessly jumps into the deep end.

Just like your father.

I get up and join him.

It's late afternoon when I hear Lev's knock, the three taps, a pause, then one more. I get up from the bed where I'm watching the door while Josh is wholly absorbed by the TV and unlock the bolt from inside.

"Thank God," I say, melting into Lev's arms as soon as I see him, that knot in my stomach finally coming undone.

"Daddy!" Josh comes charging off the bed and launches himself against Lev's legs.

"This might be the best greeting I've ever had," Lev says, lifting Josh with one arm and hugging us back.

We walk into the room, and Lev closes the door behind him. I step backward. He sets Josh down and rustles his hair.

"Did you just take a bath?"

"Mommy and me went swimming."

He looks up at me.

"I sent you a text. Didn't you get it?"

"Shit." He pulls his phone out of his back pocket and walks to where the chargers sit on the table. He plugs his in and puts it down. "I didn't have my phone on me for most of the day, and by the time I got it back, it was out of charge."

"Did it go okay?" He's in one piece.

"Yeah," he says. "Better than expected, actually."

"Daddy, look at my suit!" Josh comes running out of the bathroom where I'd hung our suits up to dry.

He's carrying his suit, the ball, and one of the floats, all still soaking wet.

"Oh, those are nice."

"Minions," Josh points out.

Lev crouches down.

"And I got a ball and floaties and Mommy got a suit, but hers is only pink." That last part he attempts to say in a whisper because I guess that's *bro code*.

"I bet she looked beautiful in it," Lev says, standing again.

"I charged it all to the room. I hope that was okay?" I ask.

"Of course. Don't even think about it." He comes to me with Josh's wet things in his hand as Josh returns to the TV. "Come with me and let's hang these up."

We go into the bathroom, and he closes the door most of the way, then drops the ball and floaty in the tub and hangs the suit on the heating rack beside mine. He picks mine up, examines the skimpy suit, and raises an eyebrow.

I take it from him and put it back to dry. "It was the least expensive one."

"I can see why. There's not much to it."

"Well, don't worry, it was pretty much just families with their kids."

"And I'm sure the dads got a hard-on looking at your ass in this."

"Shut up," I tell him, playfully slapping his arm.

He catches me by my waist and pulls me to him, squeezing an ass cheek in his hand.

"You good? You weren't scared?" he asks.

I shake my head. "It was okay. I was worried about you, though, and I'm glad you're back. Why didn't you have your phone?"

"Gleb took them during our meeting."

"Why?"

"Pretty normal for a man at his level."

"Tell me about it." I'm anxious to hear about his meeting with Gleb. I still haven't quite wrapped my brain around the fact that he's my father, and I can't see myself accepting it as easily as Josh has accepted Lev.

"It went well. He got one look at a photo of you, and you should have seen his face. I do think he cared about your mother. I could see it on him and feel it when he found out she'd been killed."

Tears fill my eyes. "I'm glad. I know it sounds weird, but—"

"It doesn't sound weird." He hugs me, then kisses my forehead. "He wants to meet you, Kat."

I draw back and look up at him. I knew he'd want that. Of course, he would. But I'm not remotely prepared.

"Does that mean he believes I'm his daughter?"

"I don't know. I mean, he's done the math, I'm sure, but I guess there's a chance you're not."

He doesn't want to say there's a chance my mom had more than one lover. I don't either, but I understand.

"When?"

"Tonight. Before dinner."

"Before dinner? That's now."

He checks his watch. "Yeah."

"What about Josh?"

"He'll come with us. I'm not trusting him with anyone."

"Maybe Maxim can watch him?"

"I trust Maxim but no. He'll come with us."

"Are you sure it's safe? I mean, what if he thinks I'm not his daughter and—"

"He gave me his word. We have to trust it. And I wouldn't take you if I didn't feel it was safe."

"What about Vasily?"

"He's MIA."

"That tip to the cops about the body?"

"Bastard had it cleaned up. The body was gone. No trace of the girl in the ground or in the house. Although there was CCTV footage of Andrei leaving with her so there's that at least."

"Will Gleb help us with Vasily?"

"If he believes what we told him today, he'll more

than help us. He'll put a hit out on my uncle himself."

"And if he doesn't believe you?"

"Let's go meet him. I think we'll know then where we stand."

"I'm scared, but I trust you. And..." I pause, remembering what he'd said earlier. "I love you, too, you know?"

He pulls me to him to kiss him just as we hear a knock on the door.

I freeze, but Lev springs into action.

He's gone in a second, and by the time I get to the bedroom, I see Josh standing at the open door looking up at a woman. Lev is beside him, hand on Josh's shoulder, one leg almost blocking Josh's view of the stranger.

"I brought towels, sir. We didn't clean the room today."

"Thank you," he says and takes them.

A moment later she's gone, and I can breathe again.

Lev turns to Josh.

"When someone knocks, you let Mommy or me open the door, okay?" His voice is tight even though he's trying to sound more casual than I know he feels.

Josh looks at him in confusion, then his lower lip

begins to tremble because he must sense this shift in Lev's mood too.

"You're not in trouble, Josh," I say, gathering him up in my arms. "It's just that we have to be careful with strangers, that's all."

He nods, burying his face against my chest.

Lev straightens, puts the stack of towels on the bed, and looks at his watch.

"We need to go, Kat. The car should already be here."

16

KAT

Josh and I sit in the back of the SUV while Lev rides in front. I'm anxious as we weave through rush-hour traffic, the driver not saying a word and Lev texting something into my phone. Since his was dead, he left it in the room charging and took mine.

"I'm hungry, Mommy," Josh says.

"We'll get you something to eat soon," I tell him. He hasn't eaten since our late lunch, and I don't have a snack with me.

"We're almost there," Lev says, turning a little.

I nod, biting my lip. A few minutes later, the SUV comes to a stop, and both Lev and the driver climb out. The driver opens my door, and I slip out. Lev grabs Josh up in his arms and keeps hold of him. We walk toward the two men standing beside the door.

"Bag," the one says to me.

I'm confused, and I look back at Lev who nods. I open my bag for him to look inside. Lev took the gun and placed it in the hotel safe before we left.

After looking through my bag, the man tells me to stretch my arms out.

"I'm going to get Josh a pretzel. We'll be right back," Lev says, signaling for me to do as they say while distracting Josh.

I watch how he keeps Josh's head turned away as the men search me. Once they're satisfied, I watch Lev and Josh return, Josh chomping on a huge soft pretzel.

"Why don't you and Josh wait inside? I'll be right there," he tells me, handing Josh to me. I know Lev is armed, and I guess they'll take his gun and cell phone from him like he said they'd done earlier.

I wait just inside the door the man opens, and a moment later, Lev joins us. He takes Josh from me, and his hand rests on my back as I follow the man through the busy club to a staircase at the back. I glance at Lev again before descending, and he gives me his nod.

Downstairs is quiet. There's a bar here too, but far fewer people are in this one, and all are men.

I know instantly which one is Gleb. I'd know this was the man in charge even if I weren't here knowing what I know because he radiates power.

He's older than I expect because he'd have to have been at least twenty years older than my mom. He's tall, too, as tall as Lev. I see it when he stands and buttons his suit jacket, dark eyes zeroed in on me.

"Lev?" I hesitate, turn.

"Go on, Kat." He takes my hand, and when we get closer, Gleb pulls out a chair and looks at Josh. Although I can't read the man, I swear surprise crosses his features.

"Katerina," Gleb says when I get as far as I can, the only thing between us the chair. He searches my face, takes in my dye job, which I admit is a little messy, but I didn't have the luxury of time. His eyes are intense, and he almost smiles as though he's just thought of something. "Turn around."

"What?"

"I need to see something."

I turn my head, not sure what he wants, but then I feel his hand at my hair, brushing it away from the back of my neck before pushing my sweater down a little. That's when I realize what he's looking for.

He makes a sound, and I turn back to face him.

"Every member of my family has that same mark. Looks better on a woman," he says with an attempt at a joke, but I get the feeling this meeting is heavier on him than he expected.

The mark he's talking about is the heart-shaped

birthmark on my back, just below my neck. Josh has it too in exactly the same place.

"Mommy." Josh's voice is small. He's nervous.

I turn to find him extending his arms to me, so I take him from Lev.

Gleb looks at Josh, and Josh looks back at him. Josh's hair is a shade darker than Lev's, and I wonder if that's from Gleb's side.

"He has it too," I say, and Gleb looks back to me, eyebrows raised. "The birthmark."

Gleb smiles, then looks at Josh's pretzel. "What is that? Are you hungry, boy?"

"Josh. His name is Josh."

"Are you hungry, Josh?"

Josh buries his face in my neck.

"Sit down," Gleb says and calls someone over.

I sit with Josh on my lap, and Gleb's eyes go from me to Josh and back like he can't quite believe what he's seeing.

"What do you want to eat?" he asks Josh. "They'll make you anything you want."

Josh looks at me.

"No marshmallow pancakes," I tell him with a wink.

He smiles and turns to Gleb. "Chicken nuggets."

"Chicken nuggets." Gleb shakes his head. "Get the boy some chicken nuggets and put something green next to them."

"He won't eat green," I interrupt. "Carrots maybe?"

"Carrots. Put some carrots next to them. What about a drink, Josh?" It's like he's trying out the name.

"Coke," Josh says.

"You're pushing it," I say.

He looks from me to Gleb and adds a, "Please."

Gleb grins and nods. "Polite. Very good. A Coke for the boy. And bring my vodka. Are you hungry, Katerina?"

"Um, no thanks."

He nods to dismiss the man who disappears then reappears a moment later with a bottle of vodka. I have never heard of this brand, but I gather from the decorative bottle it's a fairly exclusive one. Gleb pours for Lev and me without asking if we want it, but honestly, I could use it.

We sit in awkward silence while Gleb watches me, drinking three times the vodka I manage to.

When the chicken nuggets come, Lev takes Josh to sit on his lap, and Josh starts to eat.

Gleb watches him for a long minute. "He's yours?" he asks Lev.

"Yes."

Gleb nods, then turns to me.

"She named you after my sister," he finally says. "They were good friends."

"They were?" I suddenly feel so sad. I know nothing about my mother. Not one thing

"She died young too. Cancer. One year before your mother...was forced to leave." His voice hardens at the end, and he pours himself another vodka, his grip hard on the bottle.

"I don't know anything about her. I don't remember anything."

"I'll tell you. Don't worry. But we need to discuss other things first. You'll stay at my home with the boy—"

"No. They stay with me, and we stay where we are," Lev says, his voice authoritative and uncompromising. He reaches under the table to take my hand.

Gleb looks irritated by this, and I get the feeling not many people tell him no. He turns to me.

"I don't know you," I start before he can say anything. "Josh has had enough upheaval in his life this past week. I can't change one more thing."

He considers my words and then nods. "For the time being." He touches my hair. "You changed your hair. It's the same color as Ciara's?"

I nod.

"For that bastard Vasily, you did it?"

I snap my gaze to Josh.

"Sorry, sorry," Gleb says, waving off his words and drinking more of his vodka. "You need protection. The hotel—"

"Lev protects us. We're fine."

Gleb looks at Lev with a raised eyebrow. Josh finishes his last chicken nugget and picks up his Coke. It looks out of place here, the plastic sippy cup with its brightly colored cartoon characters on it and the bright yellow straw. He slurps the last of his soda and puts down his cup.

"You like to play games, Josh?" Gleb asks.

Josh nods, feeling more relaxed after being fed exactly what he wanted, I guess.

"Dima," Gleb calls. A man comes over. "Take Josh to play one of those games."

I look at where he's pointing at some machines that seem to be a throwback from the 90s.

"Looks like they have Pac-Man," Lev says to Josh who doesn't know what Pac-Man is.

"Want to play?" I ask Josh.

"With you." He casts a still unsure glance at Gleb.

"I'll be right here. You can see me the whole time, and I can see you, okay?"

He nods, but I see it takes him a minute to slip his hand in Dima's even though Dima is attempting a smile. I wonder if I should tell him it's better if he doesn't.

"He'll be fine," Gleb says.

Lev and I both turn back to him. He leans toward me and pushes my hair back from my face. He's closer than I expect, and it takes a moment for me to remember not to pull back. He runs his thumb over the healing yellowing bruise.

"Andrei Stanislov did this? Laid a hand on you? That bastard, Vasily, knew she was pregnant and put a hit on her. He knew I had a child, and he didn't tell me." He shakes his head as if in regret. "All these years. A grandchild too." He reaches into his pocket and takes out his phone. Someone answers immediately. "Any word on that rat?" I can hear the disgust in his voice.

He nods, mutters something under his breath.

"I want them both. Alive."

17

LEV

"I have something I want to show you." Gleb gestures for me to follow him out back. It's late, past midnight, and I don't like leaving Kat alone at the hotel, but at least Maxim is in the lobby, keeping an eye out for me. I just hope he stays sober enough to recognize any problems that might pop up.

"Don't worry so much." Gleb waves off my concerns. "I got a couple of my guys parked outside of the hotel. If they see anything, I'll be the first to know."

It shouldn't surprise me that he's already figured out where we're staying. New York is Gleb's turf, and he's got eyes and ears everywhere. Still, they are guys I don't know.

"You should have spoken to me first," I tell him.

Gleb stops, meeting my gaze in challenge. "Are you telling me I need to ask permission from you to protect my own daughter? My grandson?"

I consider my words carefully but refuse to back down on this. "She might be your daughter, but she's my future wife. And I look out for both of them. I don't know your guys. Kat doesn't know your guys. You need to understand that she didn't grow up in this life. If she sees a couple of bozos speaking Russian, the first thing she's going to do is run. That's all her experience has taught her."

Gleb is quiet, his face unmoving, and I can't tell if he's going to club me over the head or finish the conversation. He doesn't give a lot away. I can see now why Ciara would have been worried about coming to him and confessing her sins. But I also know that he can be softer than his reputation. I saw it with Kat. And I saw it when I mentioned Ciara too.

"You make a valid point." He shrugs. "I'll give you that. The last thing I want to do is scare her off. But you need to understand that being her father, and the man that I am, I have a say in what goes on in her life. That includes you. Now, I can respect a man who stands up for his family, but if you want to deem yourself worthy of my daughter, you have more work to do."

He steps away from me and continues toward the

door, leaving me to follow without any resolution to the conversation. This is the way of a mafia boss, and Gleb owns it. He doesn't have to wait for me. He doesn't have to respect me as a man, a husband, or a father. And even if I've known Kat longer than he has, he also has the right as her father to tell me to fuck off. Not that I will, but he has that right.

I don't know Gleb well, but I think he's a man I can respect. He doesn't fly off the handle when he's challenged like Vasily would. He listens, and he can be reasonable. And at the end of the day, I want his acceptance of my relationship with Kat. Because with a man like Gleb, you're either with him or you're against him.

The back door to the club swings open, and at least five of his men are waiting for us outside. Their faces are a mask of indifference as they allow him to speak first.

"You get me what I wanted?" Gleb glances at the van that's been backed up to the club.

"Yes, boss. You want it now?"

Gleb nods, and one of the guys gestures to the driver in the van. A second later, both front doors open, and a couple of guys dressed in scrubs step out. I look at Gleb, but he gives nothing away as they walk around to the back of the van and open the doors, revealing a hospital bed.

It takes me a minute to recognize what I'm

seeing. The parking lot is dimly lit, but I can make out the familiar face as four of the guys work as a team to offload the bed and wheel it toward us.

"Andrei?"

I can't help the grin that curves across my face as they get closer. He's as quiet as a church mouse, but that's probably because they've wrapped a shit load of duct tape around his mouth. His hands and feet are also bound together, and it already looks as though he's had a hell of a day. Or a hell of a month, more accurately.

"Take him down to the basement," Gleb commands.

The guys nod and wheel the bed inside, and I shake my head, a little impressed by the reach that this man has.

"How the hell did you get him out of the hospital?" I ask.

"This isn't my first rodeo." Gleb smirks. "Now, let's get down to business, shall we? You want to prove yourself worthy of my daughter?"

I arch an eyebrow at him. "I am worthy," I assure him. "But I'm willing to prove it if that hasn't already been made clear."

"You're a cocky son of a bitch." He narrows his eyes. "I'm sure I don't have to remind you what he did to Kat."

"No, you don't." My voice hardens. "I remember it clearly."

Gleb closes the door behind us and leads us back to the stairs. "Then make him pay for it. I want to see exactly what she means to you."

I DOUBT anybody would suspect that in the basement of one of New York's most exclusive clubs is a room that could easily rival a torture chamber. I've never been a real creative guy, but as I look around at all the instruments at my disposal, my pulse thrums with possibilities.

Gleb is parked in the corner, vodka in hand, watching me as I make my first selection. It's a sanding machine in an alternate universe, but in ours, it's better known as a human meat grinder.

"First order of business." I set the grinder down on the table beside Andrei's hospital bed and grab a pair of scissors. "I want to see what we're working with here."

I cut the hospital gown away from his body in bits and pieces, leaving him stark naked and shivering. He can't move an inch, his arms and legs bound to the rails of the bed, but his eyes are free to roam over my face as I examine the nub where his dick used to be. There are still stitches along the skin they've managed to piece together, and it's a gruesome sight to behold.

"Ouch." I shudder. "Did quite a number on you, didn't I, Andrei?"

He mumbles something beneath the duct tape, but I shake my head and tap his face.

"I've heard quite enough out of you over the years. And I'm long past giving a fuck what you have to say."

I reach for the grinder, and he starts to squeal as I look around his body for an area that will bring maximum pain. There are a lot of different nerves in the body, easily provoked, but I think the easiest route is the still healing bullet wound in his shoulder.

"This is for Kat." I meet his gaze as I flip the switch, and despite his mouth being covered, Andrei manages to scream like a banshee as blood sprays across both of our faces. I don't stop until I see bone and his blood is mixed with the salt of his own tears.

When I'm finished with his shoulder, I move onto his face. The face he always thought so highly of. I know this will hurt him the most. Apart from his own dick, I would say it was his most valuable asset.

But even as his blood drips down my wrists, it doesn't give me the satisfaction I'd hoped at seeing him cut up like a pig at a butcher shop. Because in my mind, I can still picture Kat, lying on the floor of the safe house with her pants pulled down around her knees. Face bruised, tears streaking her cheeks, while my son screamed upstairs, terrified.

My blood pressure rises as I toss the grinder aside and reach for a hammer, starting in on the small bones first. Fingers, wrists, feet. I smash them all until they are so deformed, he'd never be able to use them again, if I was kind enough to let him live. But this fuse has been lit for a long time. I've wanted to put Andrei down for years, before I even knew the full extent of what he was capable of. It isn't difficult to recall all the faces of the people he's destroyed. The lives he's fucked up. The pain he's caused.

Somewhere along the line, those faces bleed into my mother, and his words come back to haunt me. How he touched her. How she vomited. I want Andrei to feel that pain. I want him to feel as sick as I do every time I think about it.

Gleb shoots me a curious look when I reach for the broom and pry Andrei's legs apart. At some point, while I was torturing him, his screams turned to faint moans. But he manages to find the energy for another horrific yelp when I shove the broom handle up his ass.

"I bet that medicine is bitter." I lean down into his face and impale him again. "I bet it fucking hurts, doesn't it? Is that what my mother said to you? Did you even listen? Did you even care?"

His eyes roll back in his head, and I know he's on the verge of passing out. Too much of a pussy to take what he's given so freely in this world. I grab him by the face and slap him around a couple of times, forcing him to wake up.

"We aren't done yet," I roar into his face. "We aren't even fucking close. You think you're checking out? Think again, motherfucker."

My fist slams into his throat, and he chokes on the air that gets trapped in his lungs, wheezing and coughing, and then eventually gurgling. I draw my hand back to do it again, and that's when I feel a hand on my shoulder. It's Gleb.

"Lev." His voice carries an undercurrent of sympathy. "Finish him. You've proven your point."

Andrei's head falls back against the bed as his hair slips from my grasp. And I look down at him, stunned by the violence still churning inside me. Violence and rage I didn't even know the depths of until this moment. But one glance at Gleb, and I can tell it's too much even for him.

"Finish him." He hands me his pistol. "And be done with it."

"You never mentioned he killed your mother too," Gleb says.

"I know." I finish wiping my face with the towel he gave me and sit down at the bar beside him, where he already has a large glass of vodka waiting for me.

"I've been in this business for a long time." Gleb spins the glass around in his hand. "Let me tell you something. Revenge is necessary, but it can also be a poison. You have to make your peace when it's done. Let it go. Move on. Do you understand what I'm saying?"

"I understand."

My gaze drifts to the wall, and I think about Kat back at the hotel, completely unaware of what I'm capable of. Or maybe she is aware, but she chooses to see past it anyway. It fucking hurts, loving someone so much. Wanting the best for them, but being torn between two worlds, and I think if anyone can understand that, it's Gleb.

"You don't have your stars," he notes. "You were never inducted?"

"No." I shake my head. "My father wasn't a Vor. Vasily just wanted me to do his bidding. He never asked me to swear an oath, and I never offered. It was what it was."

Gleb seems to consider this for a moment, and I worry that he's going to suggest I swear that oath now. For better or worse, we're linked for life by the woman I love. The woman I promised I would give a better life to.

"Truth be told, I don't know if I'd do it again," Gleb admits. "And I don't want this life for my daughter. She deserves better than a man she can't be sure will come home every night."

"I don't want that for her either." I meet his gaze. "And I promised her it wouldn't be that way."

"That's a lofty promise to make," he says. "But I want you to fulfill it. When this shit with Vasily is done, that's it. You turn legit, and when we see each other, it will be at a family gathering. You understand?"

"Does that mean I have your approval?" I smirk.

"If Kat says she wants to marry you, then you have my approval." He nods. "But first, let's worry about finishing the job we started."

"Any word on Vasily?" I ask.

"No." He shrugs. "But I just had my guys send all of his contacts a text with a photo of Andrei. So I doubt it will be long now before he makes an appearance. When he does, I need to know if there are any more surprises, Lev. No more secrets. Not between family."

I drain the rest of the vodka from my glass and allow the burn to soothe my raw throat before I turn to him. "I'll give you everything I have on him. But I'm keeping copies for myself until this is over."

Gleb nods and then reaches for the vodka. "Very well. I'll come by the hotel tomorrow to pick it up. We can spend the day together. As a family."

18

KAT

I wake to a tickle on my neck. Scratching the spot, I then settle back into sleep, but a moment later, it's there again.

My eyelids flutter open to take in the lights peeking around the closed curtain, then close. I roll onto my back, and when the blanket slips from me, I reach to pull it back. When I meet with resistance, I open my eyes, thinking it slid to the floor.

That's when I see him.

"Lev," I say sleepily.

I move to sit up, but he bends down, splaying my thighs open as he takes hold of the crotch of my panties and pushes them over.

A moment later, his mouth closes on my sex, and I suck in a breath at the heat of it, the wet warmth of his mouth, his soft tongue. He's hungry, and I fist the sheets as he works his tongue over me, devouring me. He lifts his head to scratch the scruff of his jaw against the hard nub of my clit and slides two fingers inside me, hooking them, finding...fuck...just that spot.

I think I hear him chuckle as he covers my mouth with his hand when I begin to moan, arching my back, coming on his tongue.

When Lev fucks me, he's hard. Rough.

When he eats my pussy, it's all soft and wet, and oh my God, I need him to stop.

"Please!"

He draws his fingers out, then drags my panties off before laying his weight on me, elbows on either side of my head.

"I like how you taste, Kat," he says, then kisses me with lips still wet from me.

I taste myself on him and meet his tongue with my own as I reach down to undo his jeans. I'm hungry too. I need him.

He straightens to straddle me, and I watch him pull his shirt over his head, greedy when I see his naked chest, shoulders, and arms. I lick my lips and grab at his partially opened belt.

"I'm going to have to eat your pussy every night before bed," he says, unzipping his jeans and fisting himself.

He pumps once, twice, and I'm unable to drag my eyes away.

I reach out, run my finger along the wet tip and bring it to my lips, smearing it on like it's lip gloss before licking it off to taste him.

"More," I demand.

"You're a dirty girl," he says with a grin. He slides off the bed to strip off his jeans and briefs, then kneels over me again, this time trapping my arms at my sides.

"More?" he asks. Jerking himself off, he touches the head of his cock to my lips.

I nod, opening my mouth to take him. He grips the headboard with one hand as he leans over, looking huge above me as he guides his cock into my mouth.

"Eyes on me," he says, setting his other hand on the wall. "I want to watch you take me."

He moves slowly at first, but I can feel the urgency building, and when he hits the back of my throat, I gag. He draws back and lets me catch a panting breath before going in again.

"You're not ready for me to fuck your face yet, Kat, not the way I want to," he finally says before drawing out. He slides over me and cups my face to kiss my mouth.

"I want—"

"I know what you want," he says and kisses me

again. He closes his hands over my thighs and bends my knees up. "But what I need right now is to fuck you the way I need to fuck you."

He lifts up and looks down at me like this, everything open and exposed to him. He licks his lips.

"You're fucking beautiful." He pushes my knees wider and thrusts into me, forcing the breath from me. "And so fucking tight."

He's rough when he fucks me, the opposite of his mouth.

"Christ." He draws out, keeping my legs wide as we both look at where his cock glistens. "Get on your hands and knees," he tells me, but he doesn't wait for me to move. Instead, he flips me over and hauls my hips up, forcing my knees wider than is comfortable and splaying my ass open before dipping his head down to lick my pussy. There's that soft again, but it's gone in an instant, and he grips a handful of hair and tugs my head backward as he drills into me.

My back arches, and I slip one hand between my legs to play with my clit. The sound of our fucking is loud and wet, skin slapping against skin, his groans and my moans, and when I feel him thicken, feel that familiar twitch just before he comes, I come too, my walls pulsating around him as if to milk him. He thrusts one final time and stills deep inside me, throbbing, emptying into me.

When it's over, we both collapse. Him behind me, one arm heavy around my waist.

I move to go to the bathroom and clean up, but he tugs me closer.

"I want my smell on you. My cum inside you." He slips his hand down over my belly and cups my pussy, smearing what's leaked out into me, the sensation too much for my still sensitive clit. "I'm going to put another baby in you, Kat."

I quell the hope that creeps up at his words. It's too early to say yet, so I don't say anything. Instead, I lie on my back and turn to him. In the light coming in from around the curtains, I can see his face. I brush back his unruly hair and run my palm along his scruffy chin.

He leans down, and I meet him halfway to kiss him. It's a long, soft kiss, and it makes me think we have time. That time is maybe finally on our side.

When he draws back, he lies on his side and looks at me. He fingers a lock of my hair.

"Can you wash the black out?"

"Does that mean it's safe?"

He gives the tiniest tilt of his head as he considers, and I think I have my answer. *No. Not yet.*

"What did Gleb want with you?" I ask.

He shifts so he's lying on his back, and it's like he shutters himself off. He's done this before, in the very beginning that morning at his house.

"Just some business. Nothing you need to worry about."

I get up on one elbow and rest my head in my hand. I touch his chest, tracing the muscles over it down to his cut belly. I touch his scars too, and I think about that business. About what he's done.

"I want to know, Lev."

"No, Kat. You won't know that side. Ever."

I study him, then lay my hand flat against his chest and feel the muscle beneath it, feel the strength. I'm comforted by it.

"Do you have to work for him now?"

He looks momentarily confused. "Your father?"

My father.

"Gleb," I amend. I'm not yet ready to call him my father.

"No. Once this is done, I'm out. You, me, Josh and..." He puts his hand on my belly. "And the rest of our family will lead normal, boring lives. We'll move to Colorado if you want to go back. Hell, maybe I'll buy a pair of khakis like your boyfriend."

"Luke wasn't my boyfriend and please never buy khakis." I lie back with a laugh and close my hand over his.

"Don't worry, there's no risk of that happening."

I turn my face to watch him. "Do you mean it? Will he let us go?"

"You're his daughter. Josh is his grandson. He'll

want to be a part of that, and I won't stop him. I think that's only right. But we're not in that life anymore. That's over. As soon as my piece of shit uncle shows his ugly face, it's over."

I shudder with a sudden chill.

Lev pulls the blanket up over us.

"He's still out there? Vasily?"

Lev nods.

"His men?"

"Only someone with a death wish will have anything to do with him now."

"What about Andrei?"

"Andrei's dead, Kat," he says, his tone different. Final.

I'm quiet. I just look at him, not sure what I feel. Because Andrei deserves worse than death for what he's done. For all the lives he hurt, the lives he took. But it's still strange to hear it.

"Did he pay?" I hear myself ask because Lev may not want to tell me what he did, but I know. I've always known.

He shifts his gaze to me. He's quiet for a long minute, studying me before he answers. "He suffered. I made sure of that."

I nod. That's all I need.

"Let's get some sleep," Lev says. "Prepare ourselves for that family time with Gleb tomorrow."

I roll onto my side, and he draws me against him, tucking his legs behind mine.

"Gleb and family time. I'm not sure what to think about that."

"What did Josh say, by the way?"

"I think he's even more confused. I mean, the man did give him chicken nuggets and let him drink a Coke, so that goes a long way with Josh."

I feel him smile behind me. "The way to a man's heart is through his belly."

It grows quiet, and I listen to Lev's breathing even out.

"Lev?" I ask.

"Mmm."

I want to tell him I have a bad feeling. Like we shouldn't be celebrating just yet because it's not over. Vasily is backed into a corner. Andrei is dead. He has nothing left to lose, and that makes him even more dangerous.

But then I listen to him, and I know he's asleep, so instead of all that, I tell him that I love him.

19

KAT

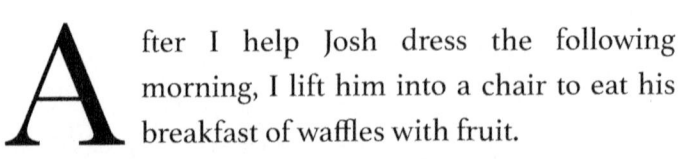

After I help Josh dress the following morning, I lift him into a chair to eat his breakfast of waffles with fruit.

Drenched in syrup.

At least there's fruit, I tell myself. And once we get home, I'll get him back on a healthy diet. The kid has a serious sweet tooth.

I'm nervously checking the time while Lev showers. Gleb is picking us up soon to have that "family day." He hasn't told us what he has planned, but I know we're going to his house, which is a little way out of the city. I've packed Josh's floats and ball in a bag as he apparently has both an indoor and an outdoor pool. His suit is still damp so I left it hanging in the bathroom to dry a little longer.

I'm not sure what I expected before I met Gleb. A

DNA test maybe. But I guess between the birthmark, my resemblance to my mother, and my age, he was satisfied.

He's not married and doesn't have other family that I know of yet. Just the sister for whom I'm named, but she's gone, so maybe he's lonely.

"Daddy's singing," Josh says with an attempt at a chuckle as he shakes his head and spoons a strawberry into his mouth.

The shower switches off, but Lev is still singing.

"He doesn't have a very good singing voice, does he?" I ask, wrinkling my nose while wiping syrup off his chin.

Josh shakes his head as the bathroom door opens.

"You guys making fun of my singing?" Lev asks with a faux-stern expression.

"You can't sing, Daddy," Josh says, then turns to watch the piece of waffle drop from his spoon onto the carpet. "Uh-oh."

"I'll clean it up. You keep eating. We have to go soon."

"Can you grab me a clean shirt?" Lev asks.

I pull the duffel bag open and take out his last white T-shirt. This is signature Lev. I notice then that the envelope he'd carried out of here yesterday morning is back in the bag.

"You didn't send it?" I ask, turning to find him

towel dry his hair while watching the cartoon over Josh's shoulder.

He turns to me. "That was a precaution. In case things went south."

"I'm glad. Here." I hand him the shirt and pick up the black one off the floor. "This isn't yours, is it?" It's the one he'd stripped off last night.

He glances at it, takes it from me, and drops it into a trash can. "I borrowed it."

I consider this, remembering what he'd said about Andrei, but I let it go.

Once Lev is dressed, he combs his hair, then takes Josh into the bathroom to wash his hands. I watch them from the bedroom. He's so natural, so relaxed, like he's always been here, like he's always been in our lives.

A ding signals a message on Lev's phone which is on the table.

Gleb: Downstairs.

"He's here."

Lev takes the phone as Josh sits to put on his shoes.

"You ready for our 'family day'?" Lev asks me.

"As ready as I'll ever be." I slip my hand into his, and we turn to Josh. He's trying to tie his laces, which he can't do just yet. "You'd think at least half the time he'd get them on the right foot," I say, noting how Josh's shoes are on the wrong feet.

Lev shrugs and goes to help Josh while I get our coats, the bag with the swim things, and my purse. Lev stops when we walk into the hallway, doubles back, then returns with the envelope in his hands a moment later, and soon, we're heading down in the elevator, the three of us looking like a normal family on the mirrored walls.

The lobby is buzzing, much like the day before. I watch Lev as he casually—or at least giving the appearance of casual—scans the lobby when we cross it. I recognize Gleb's entourage through the glass doors at the entrance even before we're outside. Three hulking black SUVs all with windows tinted so dark they're opaque.

"Oh, shoot." I stop.

"What is it?" Lev asks.

"I forgot Josh's suit. It's still drying. I'll run up."

"I'll go. You go outside."

"No, it's okay. I know where it is. I'll just be a minute," I say and walk quickly back to the elevators. One opens as soon as I get there, and I get on and push the button for our floor.

"Bye, Mommy," calls Josh.

I hear him and look up from my purse where I'm searching for the key and manage to wave to his little smiling face just before the doors close. Holding the key in my hand, I look up at the numbers as they count up, feeling how quiet it is. How strange it feels without Lev and Josh with me.

In a very short amount of time, we've grown into a family. And I don't like being away from them.

That feeling from last night comes over me again. That dread that sits like a knot in my belly.

When the elevator dings at our floor, I jump. Hurrying down the hall, I pass a housekeeper's cart and hear the vacuum cleaner going. Life goes on like normal here while I'm about to go to my mob boss father's house with my son and Lev and have some family time. So weird.

I'm thinking this as I slide my key into the lock. It doesn't work at first, the light blinking red twice. I'm about to ask the housekeeper to let me in when, the third time, I hear it click and I open the door.

I go into the bathroom to grab the suit and hope it's dry, or dry enough at least.

It's then I feel it.

That skin-crawling sensation of someone watching.

I remember the man in the woods at the school back home. That was Lev. Josh had seen him too. It's the same feeling now—but not quite.

This is more malicious.

And then I hear a sound that's grown too familiar in the last days of my life.

The cocking or de-cocking of a gun.

And when I turn, I see a man I don't know, but who looks horribly, terribly familiar all the same. Like Andrei's face on an older man. It's the gleam in the eyes, I think. The hate inside them.

"Expecting your boyfriend?" he asks, and before I can even open my mouth to scream, he lifts the gun and slams it into my temple.

The pain is instant and shattering. I fall forward, almost catch myself on the sink, but I crash into the mirror, breaking it. Another blow comes to the back of my head, and this time, I don't feel pain. Not when he hits me. Not when my mouth slams against the lip of the sink as I go down. Not when I taste my own blood as Vasily kicks me in the ribs just before I pass out.

20

KAT

I smell car exhaust as I fight to clear the fog I'm lost in. My head throbs like never before and I hear myself groan. I want to sleep. To escape. But I know I have to wake up. I have to fight.

"Put her in the trunk and get lost."

I'm dropped and hit something hard. The jolt has me opening my eyes, but all I see is darkness.

Panic surges through me. Josh.

Does he have Josh?

No. He doesn't. Does he? I was alone upstairs. I'd forgotten Josh's swimsuit. That's why I'd gone back.

Josh.

"Bye, Mommy." I hear his sweet little voice and see his tiny face between the closing elevator doors again.

Is that it? Is that the last time I'll see him?

God. I'm going to be sick.

"I said get lost and make sure you stay lost, fuckhead."

Vasily.

I turn my head, look up to see two faces. Vasily's is one, and the other man looks like a terrified junkie as he meets my eyes.

Vasily shoves bills at him, and a moment later, he's gone.

Not too terrified to aid and abet in a kidnapping.

"You're awake, good," Vasily says, lifting my arms, bringing my wrists together and holding them in one of his as he picks up a roll of duct tape and starts to wind it around my wrists too tightly.

"Hurts," I manage, my tongue feeling thick, my lip thicker.

"Does it?" He grins, drops my arms and the tape. "I'm just getting started." He raises his arm, and I see the butt of the gun before he smashes it into my skull again.

My brain rocks, and my eyes close. The last sound I hear is the slamming of the trunk.

When I come to again, I'm not in the trunk anymore. I'm moving. Well, someone is moving, and I'm over their shoulder.

I taste puke. I must have thrown up at some point. My head hurts like my skull's being squeezed in a vise. I open my eyes and even that hurts. I can't lift my head but watch the ground as we move indoors into a large, dark space. I must lose consciousness again because when I next wake, I'm sitting on a chair, being taped to it as my head lolls to the side. I'm sure I'd fall over if it wasn't for the tape.

My hair is matted with blood—mine—and when I look down at my bound hands on my lap, I see that some of my fingernails are torn. The pinky of my right hand is broken. I can tell from the angle, not so much the pain because everything hurts, and I can't figure out what's worse.

The sound of tape finally ceases, and he grips a handful of my hair to force my head up.

I look at him, at Vasily Stanislov's face. Lev's uncle.

This is the man who killed my mother.

The same man who killed Lev's mother.

He looks like he hasn't shaved in days, and his hair is matted and greasy. His clothes, too, look worn, and from the smell, he hasn't showered in a few days.

He doesn't look like Lev, I think. There's something different inside Lev's eyes. Or maybe that's just how he looks at me.

"You don't look so hot now," he says, and I wonder if my ears are damaged because his voice echoes at first, but then the room sways around him too so maybe it's not my ears but my brain that's damaged.

He lets go of my hair, and I hear him walk away behind me.

My head bobs down before I can force it back up.

I'm in a huge space. A warehouse. A deserted one. Dust-covered machinery lines the walls, the floor was torn up in places, and most of the windows high up blown out. Graffiti marks many of the walls, and I think that black spot on the floor a little farther is where someone once made a fire. Maybe homeless people trying to stay warm.

There's a dripping sound in the distance and something else. Something like rushing water.

No, not water. Traffic. Which means people.

We're not completely isolated. If I can get out—

"You go by Kat or Katie or what?"

He's not far behind me, but when I try to turn to look at him, an almost electrical pain shoots down my spine, and I can't.

My thought of escape fades. I can't even turn my head. To run, even if I could get out of the chair he's taped me to, would be impossible. Not that I'm getting out of the chair. There's duct tape layered around my chest and shoulders and again at my legs binding me to it.

"I could smash your head in with this and be

finished with it, you know?" he asks me as he comes back into view holding a brick in his hand.

I eye that brick, lick my lips, and try to swallow so I can talk.

"But what would be the fun in that?" he asks, dropping it to the ground. The *thunk* it makes when it lands makes me wince.

"My mother." I need information. Anything. And I need to buy time for Lev to find me. Because he must be looking for me by now. He'll find me. Won't he? He and Gleb will find me. They have to.

Hot tears sting my eyes.

What if they do, and it's too late, and he kills Lev too? Or both of them. What will happen to Josh?

"Aww. Poor baby. Are you sad?" He brings his face inches from mine, tilting it to the side, feigning concern.

He's going to kill me. I know it.

This won't end well for me.

"Are you scared, *Kat*?"

"You killed my mother." My voice has steel in it. I don't know how. Maybe the hate I feel for this man gives me strength.

"I did. Yes. She was a two-bit whore, though. No great loss."

His words are so careless, so unfeeling. A lost human life is no great loss? My mother's life?

I draw my head back and do the only thing I can bound as I am. I spit in his face.

It lands square on his cheek, and I know he didn't expect that. And I know the moment he straightens up that I'll pay for it. Using the back of his hand, he wipes my spit away, and when he meets my eyes again, I see pure rage.

He uses the hand he just wiped his face with to slap me. It comes down so hard across my cheek that it sends my chair falling over, and my head bouncing off the concrete floor. Everything goes dark again, and I think this is it. This must be it.

"Although..." he starts. Hauling my chair upright again, he takes my face in both hands to make me look up at him. My vision is fading, though. Coming and going. "It's not like she worked the streets. She was the kind of whore who only fucked men with money. Stay with me, Kat." He gives my face two lighter slaps. "Or this won't be much fun. I'll tell you what." He steps away, and I try to look up at him. "I'll give my nephew a call. Get him on his way. The way things are looking, you aren't going to be hanging on for much longer."

He walks away, and my head droops, my eyes closing. I taste blood when I lick my swollen, tender lip, and I can't open one eye at all anymore.

I hear him talk.

And then I hear Lev.

I make a sound. I want to tell him to take care of Josh. To tell Josh that I love him and that I'm sorry. But all I can manage is a low moan. I can't even lift my head anymore.

"Where were we?" Vasily asks.

Again, I'm not sure how long I've been out because he's tapping my face to get my attention.

"That's right, your mother. She was a high-end escort."

What?

"Did you know that? Somehow, she got connected with Katerina Mikhailov, though. Maybe at a club or something, who knows? And then she met Gleb. How do I know this, you ask? Or you would ask if you could talk." He chuckles at his own joke. He has his hand in my hair again, tugging my head backward. "I said stay with me, for fuck's sake. You don't want me to have to go get your little boy, do you?"

I shake my head and try to say Josh's name, but it comes out as a gurgle of blood that drips down my chin.

"What's that? Got your attention? Josh, right? Cute kid. Looks like my side of the family."

"Stay away..."

"That's how I got her to do it, you know," he continues, pulling up a chair to sit across from me.

"Told her I'd tell Gleb about her past. He wouldn't want to be fucking a prostitute, after all."

My mother was a prostitute?

"I mean, who knows if you're even his. She'd spread her legs for anyone who looked twice."

He stands then and cocks his head to the side.

"Your boyfriend sure is taking his time, isn't he? Let's keep this interesting," he says, coming to me, pulling my head back.

"Open your eyes and look at me. I want you to see me when I do this."

I don't have control of myself, though. Doesn't he know that?

"Think about Josh. I know I am."

That makes my good eye open, and I see his wicked grin.

"Just in case things go south, this one's for him," he says. He smashes a fist into my belly so hard, it knocks the breath from my lungs and would send the chair toppling backward if he didn't have me by my hair.

I can't catch my breath. The only thing holding me upright is the tape when he lets me go, and I just wheeze as I try to get air, as I try to manage this new pain.

"If my nephew managed to put another bastard in there, Kat, know that it's dead."

21

LEV

"Where is she?" Gleb gets out of the SUV idling at the curb and comes to stand beside me. "What's taking so long?"

I can hardly speak past the tension in my throat. It's been ten minutes. The elevators can get crowded around this time of day, but it doesn't feel like that's what's happening. It's the same sick feeling swirling in my gut when I headed home to my mother fifteen years ago.

She always showed up to pick me up after work even though it was only a short subway ride home. She was afraid I'd get mugged or shot if she didn't come to get me herself. But that day, I stood outside the store where I stocked groceries to help with the bills, and the seconds ticked by, one after another, until I felt like I couldn't fucking breathe.

I knew when I walked into the door of our apartment before I ever saw her. On my way home, I'd already vomited twice. It was a sickness, creeping into my veins, blackening my vision and igniting a fever I couldn't shake. The fever has returned, and my limbs are unnaturally stiff as I walk toward the elevator bank with Gleb right behind me. He's still talking, and I can't hear a word he's fucking saying.

"Josh," I croak. "Someone needs to stay with Josh."

Maxim appears out of nowhere, and I forgot that he mentioned he was going to drop by today. "I'll watch the kid, Lev. Go get your woman."

I nod, but Gleb hesitates, gesturing for his men to watch over Maxim while I punch the button to call the elevator. It feels like it takes forever. Too goddamn long. I'm about to head for the stairs when the light finally blinks, and I shove my way in through the people trying to get off. One of the passengers glares at me, holding me up.

"Excuse you!" he snaps.

"Get the fuck off!" I roar.

His eyes go wide, and he scurries away in fear while Gleb looks at me.

"Stay calm," he says, but even his voice is shaking. He feels it too.

The elevator ascends to our floor, and I push through the doors as soon as they open, my feet slapping against the floor as I count the doors. When I reach ours, I fumble with the key card, trying unsuccessfully to unlock it three times before Gleb snatches it from me.

"Let me do it."

His hand is steadier than mine, and I don't know what that says about me. I just know that I need to get to Kat. And the second the door opens, I'm calling out for her, but she doesn't answer.

Gleb and I enter the suite, our eyes darting around the empty space. He checks Josh's bedroom while I head for the bathroom. Everything looks the same way we left it; even Josh's suit is still hanging up to dry. But when my eyes drift over the mirror and the sink, I know that nothing is the same.

It hits me like a spear straight through the heart. I feel my knees colliding with the floor as I grapple with my breath. This can't be real. It can't fucking be real. But I thrust my body forward, sliding my fingers through the crimson liquid, and my stomach clenches, threatening to spill the contents of our breakfast.

Blood. Kat's blood.

"Lev?" Gleb's footsteps pause when he sees me, and when I look up at him, the color drains from his face. "What the fuck?"

"She's gone," I choke out. "She's gone."

"How could you let this happen?" Gleb howls,

shoving me back until I collapse in a heap. He bends down, clutching my collar, screaming in my face. "You let him get to her!"

I can't speak. I can't even argue. Because I shouldn't have let her go alone. I should have followed her. I should have done so many things differently. But I didn't. And now she's gone.

"You told me you would protect her!" Gleb comes at me again, and this time, he throws a punch. It hits me square in the jaw, jarring me from my grief for a split second, and before I know it, I'm punching him back.

We're in a heap on the bathroom floor, wrestling as we scream at each other when Maxim's voice interrupts us.

"Lev, snap the fuck out of it." He yanks me away from Gleb, and the old man wipes the blood from his lip while I drag a hand through my hair. And when our gazes collide again, I recognize the raw pain in his, and I know he can see it in mine.

"This isn't the way," Gleb murmurs. "We need to work together. Let's get it together. He couldn't have gotten far."

"Where's Josh?" I ask Maxim as I glance around the room, looking for any other clues.

"He's safe. Gleb's guys bought him a milkshake downstairs. He doesn't know what's going on."

"We need to get him out of here." I exit the room with Gleb and Maxim not far behind.

"My guys can take him back to the compound. Nobody can get to him there."

I hesitate, and Maxim squeezes my shoulder. "I'll go with him, Lev. If that's what you want."

"Please," I croak.

He nods, and we pile into the elevator, the silence swallowing us up as we stew in our own thoughts. I can't accept that Kat's gone. Not yet. Whatever happened to her, there's still time. That's what I keep telling myself as we step into the lobby and Gleb starts shouting orders at his men.

I find Josh sitting by the door, drinking a milkshake just like they said.

"Can we go swimming now?" he asks, eyes shining up at me with an innocence that shatters my fucking soul.

"Soon, buddy." I force myself to smile for him. "There's something I have to take care of. But Maxim is going to go with you to Gleb's house, okay? Then I'll be there just as soon as I can."

"What about Mommy?" he asks.

I choke on the lies I don't want to tell him, but Gleb saves me, kneeling beside me. "She'll be there just as soon as she can, little soldier. Don't you worry, okay? Now you go to my house. You tell the housekeeper anything you want, and she will make it for you. It's better than Disneyland, I promise."

Josh smiles and nods. "Okay."

I pick him up and squeeze him tight before handing him off to Maxim, our eyes locking with unspoken understanding.

"Take care of my boy."

"Pause it there." Gleb squints at the screen, examining the man on the hotel's security footage. The guy operating it looks scared shitless, but Gleb threw a few hundred bucks his way, and we've been staring at this goddamn thing for far too long trying to find Vasily. So far, nothing has panned out, and this could take all fucking day at this rate.

"I'm going to do another walk around," I tell him. I need to dispel some of this nervous energy building up in me like a bomb, and I can't just stand here twiddling my fucking thumbs. I know it's unlikely that Kat is still in the hotel, but right now, it's all I can do.

Gleb waves me off, and I head into the parking garage again, ransacking my mind for any ideas of where Vasily would take her. I know all of his haunts, but he's a wanted man now. His friends, his soldiers, they've all cut ties with him after Gleb ordered a bounty on his head. He's backed into a fucking corner, and he's grieving, and he could be anywhere right now.

I scan the cars again, looking for something Vasily would drive. I check for tire marks, or some other sign that Kat was here. Anything that could help. Desperation claws at me, scorching every nerve in my body. I want to slam my fist into the brick wall. I want to cut Vasily's dick off and shove it down his throat until he chokes, and then I want to bring him back to life and do it all over again.

"Come on, Kat," I whisper. "Give me a sign. Anything, baby. Please."

My phone vibrates in my pocket, and when I check the screen, it's a New York number. The organ in my chest that's merely keeping me alive right now works overtime pumping blood into my veins at a frantic pace when I slide my finger across the screen to answer.

"How does it feel?" Vasily's voice slithers across the line. "How does it fucking feel, Lev?"

"Where is she?" I growl. "Where the fuck is she?"

"Right now?" He sneers. "She's bleeding out on the floor of an abandoned warehouse. Can you guess which one? There are a lot in this city. Maybe you can still make it here in time."

"I'll fucking destroy you." My fingers grip the phone so hard it almost snaps in half. "I'll cut every appendage from your body and make you beg for death. It won't be quick. It won't be easy—"

"Neither will hers," Vasily answers. "I want you to think about what happened to Andrei. That was a fucking picnic compared to what I'm going to do to your precious fucking whore."

Emotion chokes my voice, and it takes everything inside me to try to keep a rational head. "What do you want, Vasily? Quit playing games and tell me."

"Is Gleb with you?" he asks.

"He's in the hotel."

"Show me," Vasily orders. "Put yourself on video."

I take the phone from my ear and pull up the video screen so he can see me, and within seconds, I'm met by his ugly, sneering face.

"Satisfied?" I show him the empty garage behind me.

"Get in your car and come to the address I text you. Come alone, and don't fuck with me. I have eyes on you, Lev. If you tell Gleb, I'll fucking kill her without a second thought. If you do what I say, then I'll make you a deal. Your life for hers. So long as you get here in time."

"I'll come," I tell him. "But you'll leave her alone until I get there."

"No deal." Vasily shakes his head. "Do you think

I don't know you and Gleb murdered my son? Your little bitch gets the same. Every second you waste getting here is another second I'll be torturing her. So quit fucking around and prepare to make peace with your maker. Because when I'm through with you today, there will be nothing left but scraps for the pigs."

"Text me the goddamn address," I snarl, yanking my keys from my pocket. "And think twice before you touch her, old man. Because this ends today. Me and you. Man to fucking man. Are we clear?"

The phone shifts a little, and Vasily's face disappears from the screen before an image of Kat pops up. She's bound to a chair, duct-taped across the mouth, blood coating her hair.

"Run, run," Vasily taunts. "Time's a-wasting."

The call ends before I can say anything else, and I run to the SUV, firing it up just as the text with the address comes through. I plug it into my GPS on my way out of the garage, screeching out into New York City traffic.

My nerves are shot, and the time estimate on the phone isn't doing me any favors. Vasily is ten miles away, but that could take me an hour in this clusterfuck.

"Fuck." I slam my fist into the steering wheel as traffic comes to a crawl.

My phone rings again, and this time it's Gleb. I

stare at the screen for a few long seconds before I dismiss it. Traffic lurches forward again. The streets are a goddamn nightmare. Between traffic stops, I check alternate routes, subway timetables, and walking distance. Driving is still my best bet. I try to stay calm. Two more miles. My phone keeps ringing. Gleb sends me a text.

Where the fuck are you?

I concentrate on the road, my knuckles turning white beneath my grip on the steering wheel.

Kat's alive.

The words play over and over in my mind like a mantra. I repeat them the entire way there. When I'm a block away, I find the first parking spot available and slip into it, jamming the SUV into gear and yanking the keys from the ignition.

Kat's alive.

My feet slap against the pavement as I run to the warehouse, looking for a way in.

Kat's alive.

The exit door in the back is cracked, and I slip inside. My phone rings again. The barrel of Vasily's gun taps the back of my skull as he steps out from the shadows.

"Turn it off. Now."

I turn off the phone and meet his gaze. "Where is she?"

A smile curls across his face as he points toward

the shadows. A faint moan bleeds into my ears, and I lunge forward before Vasily yanks me back.

"This was the fucking deal!" I snarl.

"We had a deal too." He spits into my face. "Loyalty? Do you remember that fucking word, you worthless sack of shit?"

"Let her go, and you can do whatever you want to me."

"The only way she's walking out of here alive is if you kill me." His face mottles with red as he digs the barrel into my scalp. "And that's not going to happen."

Vasily shoves me forward, the gun finding a home in my shoulder blade as he prods me along. "Now take a fucking seat. You're going to watch this show from the VIP section."

He shoves me across the warehouse and orders me into a chair directly opposite of Kat. But I can't fucking move. When my gaze locks onto her bruised and bloody body, my only instinct is to get to her. She's barely conscious, her eye so swollen I don't even know if she can see me.

"Kat."

She moans, and Vasily slams the butt of his gun into the side of my head, dazing me.

"I told you to sit the fuck down!" he thunders.

On instinct, I try to take a swing at him, but he jumps back, aiming the gun right at Kat's head.

"Don't even try me, you stupid fuck. I'll put a bullet in her head so fast you won't have time to blink."

I meet his gaze, forcing myself to keep my temper in check. "What. The. Fuck. Do. You. Want?"

"I told you." He looks at me with unbridled disgust. "I want to see your blood paint this floor. But first, you get to suffer. Just like Andrei suffered."

"Andrei was the biggest piece of shit and waste of human space that ever breathed on this earth," I clip out. "I did you a favor. I did the entire fucking world a favor."

The vein in Vasily's forehead throbs as he clenches his jaw, trembling with unchecked rage. I know it's not fucking smart to provoke him, but I need a distraction.

"There isn't a line you won't cross, is there?" I ask him. "Your own sister. Your own flesh and blood."

Vasily's face pales, his gaze intensifying as he studies me. "How long have you known?"

"I've always suspected." I glare at him. "You never did anything out of the kindness of your heart. You took me in and turned me into exactly what she didn't want."

"She was a fucking traitor!" The words fly from his lips with such violence, I can't believe I didn't see his hatred for her all these years. How blind I was to the fact that I'd been living with the monster all along.

"You let your filthy spawn... *touch her*. Her own fucking nephew. You sick, depraved motherfucker!"

I want him to come for me. I want him to focus his rage on me, but being the coward that Vasily is, he always chooses the easiest fight. It still fucking shocks me to witness his depravity when he grabs Kat by the hair and backhands her. Blood flies from her mouth, and it triggers every animal instinct inside me as I lunge forward, tackling Vasily to the ground. He digs the gun into my ribs and pulls the trigger, but by some fucking miracle, it jams.

"Motherfuck!" He slams his knee up into my gut, and I choke back the pain as I twist his fingers back, trying to pry the gun from his grasp.

His bones crack, and he groans as I headbutt him, dazing him long enough to grab the weapon and toss it out of his reach.

"Now we're even." I spit into his face. "So fight me like a man, you pathetic fuck."

Vasily swings his knee up again, this time hitting me in the groin. I buckle for a split second, and he thrashes me in the temple with his elbow. We're both running on pure rage and adrenaline as we grapple for dominance.

"You killed my father too." I wrap my fingers

around his throat and squeeze. "Admit it. Admit that you destroyed my entire family."

A demonic smile curls across his face as he bends my fingers back, trying to pry me off him. "Everything you have ever loved, I have destroyed, Lev. Your father, your mother, your little bitch. When this is over, they will all have died by my will. Because I'm the fucking god you could never be. I'm the true Vor. And your father was just as weak as you. He died like a pathetic fuck, gasping for breath and pleading for mercy."

I land a solid blow to his chest, knocking the wind from his lungs, and it gives me the time I need to stagger to my feet. My boot slams into his rib cage, and he curls into a ball as I stomp on his face, shattering his nose.

He chokes on his own blood as it pours into his mouth, and I kick him again and again, watching him writhe on the floor in pain as he fights to get up. But it's too late. He's already one foot in the grave, and I'm not finishing until I send him straight to hell.

"Who's your god now, motherfucker?"

Blood spatters against my face as I grab a chunk of brick and kneel onto his chest, smashing it into his skull. Rage opens up the floodgates inside me as I slam the brick into him, over and over, painting the floor with his blood.

"Who's your fucking god now?" I roar again.

"Lev." Gleb's voice snaps me out of my murderous haze as he reaches down and pries the brick from my fingers. "He's dead."

As my eyes clear, and I wipe the blood from my face, I look down at what used to be Vasily's head. But now, it's nothing more than blood and fragments of skull, his useless brains spilling out.

"He's dead," Gleb repeats.

"No." I stagger to my feet and grab the Glock strapped to my ankle.

He can't be dead. That was too easy for him. That's what I keep telling myself as I unload an entire magazine into his body, watching as he flops around like a fish on the concrete floor. I feel no satisfaction when the blood oozes from his wounds. But one word from Gleb snaps me out of it.

"Katerina."

Kat. The Glock falls from my grasp, and I turn to her. She's not conscious, but one of Gleb's men has untied her.

"We need to get her to the hospital," Gleb says. "Now."

The guy in front of her tries to pick her up, and I shove him out of the way. "No. She's mine."

With all the delicacy I can muster, I scoop her up into my arms and try to wake her, peppering her bloody face with kisses.

"Wake up, baby. I'm here. I'm here, and I'm never leaving you again. So, you can't leave me either. That's the deal."

Gleb grabs me by the arm, dragging me along out of the warehouse while he orders a couple of his guys to stay behind and clean up.

"Wake up, baby," I say again, kissing her forehead. "I'm here."

"Lev. Get in." Gleb opens the door to his SUV, and I climb in, clutching Kat against my chest.

My eyes burn, and something splashes against Kat's cheek, and that's when I realize it's coming from my eyes.

"Katya." I clutch her face in my hands. "Don't leave me, baby. I can't do this without you."

The engine in the SUV roars to life, and I don't even know what's happening right now. Gleb issues orders, and his man drives, flying like a bat out of hell to the nearest hospital. But all I can focus on is Kat. My angel. My life. I can't fucking lose her.

I don't even realize I'm saying it out loud until Gleb turns around. "You won't, son."

But how can he know that? How did he even find us?

"My guys hacked into your GPS system a week ago," he tells me, answering another question I didn't even know I said out loud. "It was a safety precaution until this blew over."

I rock Kat in my arms, stroking her hair back away from her face. Nothing else matters right now. I just need her to wake up.

"Stay with me, baby." I whisper against her temple. "You just have to stay with me."

22

LEV

Kat's hand twitches in mine, and for a second, I drag my eyes up to her face with a hope I haven't felt in days. But beneath the bandages and the wires, and the monitors beeping around her, nothing has changed.

When we arrived at the hospital, I didn't know what to expect when they made me hand her off. I just told them they had to save her. It was the only thing I could manage. After the medical staff took her away, it felt like days had passed before we finally saw a doctor. All she could tell us was that Kat had sustained a lot of head trauma, and now the entire team keeps assuring me that this medically-induced coma will reduce the swelling in her brain and give her the best chances of survival. Best, but not guaranteed. They never say that. They never say much of anything other than they are taking it one day at a time.

Beside me, Gleb sits like a sentinel, quiet and pensive. He's been here the entire time, and even though we haven't managed to say much to each other, our shared grief is enough. I'm grateful for his presence, and in a way, I find it comforting and odd. I've only known the man a short while, but it's become clear to me that his strong, steady presence is that of a father figure. He was a father before he ever knew it. And I think in some strange way, he is the father figure I'd been looking for in Vasily for half of my life.

One thing I can't regret is bringing him and Kat together. While I've been sitting here, feeling helpless, he's called every specialist on the East Coast to ensure Kat's getting the best possible treatment. Some have shown up personally while others review her medical chart from wherever they are and offer their opinions. But even though I don't doubt Gleb has assembled the best medical team in the nation, it doesn't change anything. Time. That's all they keep telling us. She just needs time.

"When this is over..." His voice stirs me from my thoughts. "I want you to get her out of this world, Lev. I don't want this life for her."

I meet his gaze, the certainty in his tone a

comfort I haven't known before. *When this is over. Not if.*

"I did what I set out to do," I answer. "I'm done. When I bring Kat home, I'm going to be the most boring fuck she's ever met in her life. I'll put on a polo, go to work, whatever it takes. I don't care. I'm leaving this chapter behind, and she's coming with me."

"Good." Gleb nods. "But don't go too far, okay? I just met her. I want to see you guys around, maybe even watch my grandkids grow up. It would be a nice change of pace for me."

"I'll have to talk to Kat." My voice is thick. "But I think she'd like that too."

"You should eat something," he grunts. "Or go take a shower. It won't do her any good to wake up and find you looking like hell."

"I can't leave her." I swallow. "Not until I know she's okay."

"It's going to take time," he says. "Remember what the doctors said?"

I do. They told us that Kat is unconscious, but she will likely have glimpses of awareness of her surroundings. She'll dream a lot and try to make sense of things in her own mind. And it's very likely that she'll hear us on occasion, so I've made it a point to tell her every day to focus on getting better. Not to worry. And I know

Gleb is right. If she's in there, listening to us like they say, she's probably yelling at me for not doing better. Taking care of myself. Going to see Josh. I'm failing at everything, and it's ripping my fucking heart out.

"I'm going to go grab a cup of coffee," I tell Gleb to appease him. "And call Josh."

He nods, and I disappear into the void of the hallway. The scent of disinfectant and crappy hospital food burns my nostrils as my shoes squeak across the floor. When I get to the cafeteria and grab a coffee, the lady at the register offers me a sympathetic smile. She's seen me every day for the past week.

"One of these days, you should try the food too, ," she suggests. "I hear it's quite the novelty."

"Thanks." I nod. "I'll think about it."

I take a seat by the window and pull the lid off my cup, letting the steam billow out while I grab my phone and pull up Maxim's number. I've never been more grateful for the old man in my entire life. If he wasn't with Josh right now, I don't even know how I'd be able to stay with Kat.

"Hey," he answers on the second ring. "The sun is out. I'm hoping that means there's good news today."

"Not yet," I tell him. "How's everything going there?"

"We're doing just fine," he answers. "Josh is

running me ragged, but it's good for an old man to be young at heart again. You want to talk to the little fella?"

"Please."

He pulls up the video chat, something Josh had to show him how to do, and I force a smile when my boy's face comes into view. He has what looks like blueberry and marshmallow smeared across his cheek, and I can only imagine what he's been eating this week. Gleb gave him free rein to order anything he wants from the housekeeper, and it looks like Josh is taking full advantage of that.

"How are you, buddy?" I ask.

"Good." He smiles. "Uncle Maxim and I are going swimming again today. He said if I beat him across the pool again, then I get ice cream."

"Uncle Maxim?"

I quirk a brow, and Maxim shrugs in the background. "It's new. I figured—"

"It's perfect," I tell him. We might have the most fucked-up family in the world, but we are a family. Just last week, I explained to Josh that Gleb is his grandfather, and he accepted it with one simple question. Could he go swimming at Grandpa Gleb's all the time?

"So, ice cream, huh?" I force my voice to be light as I examine Josh's happy face. "Are you getting any veggies in there too?"

"He's having some carrots with lunch," Maxim assures me.

Josh nods. "And chicken nuggets."

"Well, you keep holding down the fort for me, okay, buddy? I'm going to keep taking care of Mommy, but I promise I'll come to see you just as soon as I can."

"Is Mommy's owie better?" he asks, hope shining in his eyes.

Acid burns my throat as I nod. "She's still getting lots of rest so she can try to get rid of the owie."

"Can you give her a hug for me?" Josh asks. "And tell her that I beat Uncle Maxim at swimming?"

"I'll tell her," I assure him. "I love you, buddy."

He grins, blue lips stretching wide. "I love you too, Daddy."

Maxim takes the phone off video chat and gets back on the line. "Are you sure I can't bring you anything? A change of clothes? Something to eat?"

"No, I'm good. I just appreciate you staying with Josh. I feel better having him there."

Even though the threat is gone, it doesn't mean my worries are. I think when it comes to my family, I will always worry.

"Take care of yourself, kid," Maxim says. "And next time you call, give me some good news."

"I'm trying, old man."

We say our goodbyes and disconnect the line. I

drink my coffee in silence, mulling over the uncertainties of the future. I don't know what's going to happen with Kat, but I know that the doctors told me I'm going to be a father again, if Kat can sustain the pregnancy.

In any other circumstances, I'd be over the fucking moon with pride and excitement. This time was supposed to be different. We were supposed to do it together. But instead, the reality is I might be doing alone, if it ends up happening at all. And nothing about that scenario is ever going to be okay.

23

KAT

I'm floating. That's the first sensation I register. It's bright. There's light all around me but not from any source that I can see. Just bright white light.

Am I dead? I don't feel my body. I just feel myself float as if I'm supported on a puff of air.

Did I die?

Panic washes over me, and the sensation passes.

Josh.

If I'm dead, I can't be there for Josh. What if Lev's dead too? What if he ends up in foster care, and what if a couple like the Georges get him? What if...

"Shh, baby."

I'm instantly calmed by the voice. The noise I'd barely registered levels out in the background.

I look around. I'm floating again.

A glimpse of red hair catches my eye. It's fleeting. There, then gone, then back.

She's here. And even though her back is to me, I know it's her. I know. She's holding something. Cradling it. I can tell from the way she's standing.

I sit up. It takes some effort, and when I look down at myself, my hands are bruised and deathly white, and there are wires everywhere.

I shake my head, looking up at her again.

"Mom?"

She turns like she just realized I was there, and she smiles, and she's so beautiful that I feel my eyes fill up with tears. She's just like I remember from when I was little. When she'd hold me as I fell asleep and I'd hold on to her hair like Josh does to mine.

"I miss you, Mom."

"My baby girl all grown up." I hear the words even though her lips don't move.

"Am I dead?" I ask. The peaceful feeling fades again, panic filling me instead.

She tilts her head to the side and looks sad for a moment, but then she smiles again. A reassuring smile. "Don't worry. I'll take care of her," she says.

As soon as her words are out, I feel a sharp pain in my stomach. The floating sensation is gone, replaced by sound, too much sound. Machines and people and pain. Oh my god, the pain.

"She's bleeding," a woman calls out, and I hear the sudden frantic activity around me.

"Kat? Fuck. Get the fuck off me!"

Lev.

More noise. People are yelling, and Lev is yelling too.

I open my eyes, blink at the fluorescent lights, at all the activity around me, the faces of strangers, pain in my back and stomach, warmth between my legs.

"I'm here, Kat! I'm here!"

It hurts. It hurts so much.

Something pierces my arm, and the pain begins to lessen.

"Kat?"

I can follow his voice now, and I see him. I see him beyond all those faces, and he looks wrecked. Like he hasn't slept in days. Like he's been through hell.

And I remember.

"Vitals are good again."

"Sir, we need you to step out. Someone get him out of the room please. Sir, we can't help her if you're in the way."

"I'm here, Kat," he says again.

I'm alive. He's alive. Josh? Is Josh alive?

"Josh?" I croak out.

I think I see him smile. "Josh is fine. He's waiting for his mommy."

That's good.

That's okay.

My eyes close. The world begins to fade again, and I let it, but this time, it's not bright but dark, and as my consciousness begins to fade, I try to remember what happened.

I went up to our room to get Josh's bathing suit, and Vasily was there waiting for me. He took me to that warehouse. He said terrible things about my mother. He hurt me. And he punched me in my belly.

In case things go south, he'd said. And I understand what he meant.

I was pregnant.

"Don't worry. I'll take care of her."

Her.

A little girl. She's with my mom now, and Josh is safe, and I can sleep. I don't have to worry. I can just sleep.

24

LEV

"Welcome back." I squeeze Kat's hand.

She tries to speak, her throat muscles working, but the nurse shakes her head. "Give it some time, honey. You've been out for a while. We're going to get you some water, and then the doctor wants to check you over."

Her eyes move to mine, and I lean down to kiss her forehead, a silent promise that everything's going to be okay. Right now, the room is full of nurses and technicians. There's so much I want to say. There's so much I want to know. But I have to be patient.

Kat blinks and moves her gaze around the room as the rest of her body slowly starts to wake. She's weak, cold, and terrified. I can see that in her eyes. But I want her to know that I'm here.

"Here's your water." The nurse returns. "We're going to sit you up. Sip it very slowly, okay?"

Kat blinks in response, and they adjust her bed, instructing her on what they want her to do as they help her with the water. She's so small and fragile; it wrecks my heart to see her this way. Almost childlike in her demeanor and her expressions. This isn't the Kat I'm used to, and I'm still terrified the worst is yet to come.

Maybe she won't remember me. Maybe she won't even be able to speak. Maybe she won't be Kat at all. The doctors tried to prepare me for every scenario, and they said the only way to tell is time. But I'm anxious about the exam. I want to see for myself. Regardless, it doesn't matter. I don't care if she doesn't remember me, or if she doesn't know how to speak. We'll find a way to get through it just like we did with everything else.

"Welcome back, Katerina." The doctor enters with a clipboard in hand, her eyes bright and positive as she looks over Kat. "I'm Dr. Sampson, and I'll be doing your examination today."

Kat nods. It's stiff, but it's there. The smallest of movements, but it gives me hope. So much fucking hope. If she's nodding, that means she comprehends, right? I look at the doctor, but she has a good poker face. She doesn't even blink as she wheels her chair over next to Kat's bed.

"Just give me a second to look over your vitals," she murmurs and then hands the clipboard off to one of the nurses. "Okay, here we go. We're going to run through a series of tests, Katerina. Right now, it might be difficult for you to speak, so I don't want you to worry about that. If you understand, I want you to blink twice for yes. Can you do that?"

Tension creeps into my bones as I swing my gaze back to Kat, watching like a hawk as she blinks once, and then again. It feels like we just won the fucking Olympics. Internally, I'm freaking the fuck out, but the doctor is playing it cool, and I know that means there is still a lot more to figure out.

Over the next half hour, she does a series of tests with Kat. Checking her vision, her hearing, her comprehension. One test bleeds into another, and with every victory, my racing heart slows. My baby is here. She's alive. And she's kicking ass just like she's always done.

"That's enough for today." The doctor moves to the sink and washes her hands. "I'll be back tomorrow to check on you again, and we'll keep at it. But you've done very well, Katerina. I just want you to rest now, okay?"

Kat blinks twice, and I squeeze her hand. Within a few minutes, the room clears out, and it's just Gleb and me left beside her. She looks at both of us, then back at me, her face pinching with frustration. She wants to say something, but she can't.

"Josh is okay," I tell her. "He's with Maxim at Gleb's house being spoiled rotten. Don't worry, sweetheart. He's just fine."

She blinks twice and then points at her water. I hold it up for her, letting her take a couple of sips before I set it aside. Then she brings a shaky hand to her throat, clutching at it as she opens her parched lips again. Another scratchy sound forces its way out of her lips, and I shake my head.

"Your throat is tender. The doctor said—"

"Baby."

This time, I hear the word clearly even though it's barely a whisper. My heart stalls, and Gleb lays a hand on my shoulder. Neither of us knows how to navigate this situation. And I can't bear to break Kat's heart. Not after everything she's been through.

"You need to rest, sweetheart." I lean forward and kiss her on the temple. "In a couple of days, Josh might be able to come see you. But rest first."

Her face falls, and she blinks twice. I stroke her hand in mine, and within minutes, she is back to sleep again.

THE NEXT THREE days are a series of milestones. Kat

moving her hand. Kat sitting up. Kat taking her first steps with the help of two nurses, and me and Gleb as backup, just in case. It's slow and painful to watch her struggle with the simplest of things, but she tackles them as only Kat can, with a steel backbone and determination in her eyes.

I know the biggest of her motivations is seeing Josh again. But she doesn't want him to see her so weak. Words spoken from her own lips, which she's still struggling with. She can carry on a conversation, but only for so long before she needs to take a break again. Dr. Sampson explained that it's totally normal for anyone who's been through so much trauma to feel so weak, but she's confident that Kat is likely going to make a full recovery, and it's the first peace I've had in a full month. It won't be easy. There will be physical therapy to ensure Kat regains her strength and her balance, and the potential for side effects that still haven't made an appearance yet. Dr. Sampson said headaches and mood changes are just a couple of the things we need to watch out for. But right now, when I look at Kat, she's still Kat to me. Her eyes are shining with vulnerability, and pain, but also love. Love for me.

"I missed you," she whispers. "Is that weird to say?"

I bring her palm to my lips and kiss her there. "You have no idea how much I missed you, baby."

"It was so strange," she says. "Being trapped inside my own body. So helpless. I wanted to tell you I was okay, but I couldn't. And then at times, I wondered if I really was okay, or if it was all a dream. Or if I was already—"

"Don't say it." I flinch. "Please don't even say it."

She nods, and we study each other, and I know what's coming before she even brings it up.

"The baby is gone."

Pain lances through my gut, and I nod, trying to find the words to comfort her.

"I heard them talking about it," she tells me. "And then I saw my mother."

"Your mother?" I croak.

Tears fill her eyes, spilling out onto her cheeks. "She told me she was going to take care of our little girl, Lev. She told me they are together."

"I'm so sorry, sweetheart." I bury my head against her chest, clutching her body as I choke back my emotions. "I'm so sorry. I failed you. I failed all of you."

Her fingers tangle in my hair, and she strokes me the same way she often comforts Josh. It's such a simple thing, but it means everything. I thought I would never have this again, and there isn't a second of the day that goes by that I'm not questioning if I even deserve it.

"I love you, Lev," Kat murmurs. "And our love is

stronger than everything that's happened to us. I don't need you to be sorry. I just need you to be here. Forever."

I look up at her, wishing I could pull her up into my arms and curl her against my chest. There is so much I want to tell her, but for now, a promise will have to do.

"I'm going to spend every day of the rest of my life by your side, sweetheart. I'm not going anywhere."

THREE MONTHS LATER

25

KAT

Today is Josh's fourth birthday. I'm in the kitchen icing his birthday cake when he comes running in from the open sliding glass doors.

"You won't believe what we did!" he tells me. He's excited and almost out of breath from running.

I turn to catch him, bracing myself for him to barrel into me, but Lev intercepts him.

"Whoa, take it easy," Lev tells him, lifting him in his arms. I've been home, well, at Gleb's house, for two months now, and I swear Lev's like a ninja, keeping one eye on me and always ready to spring into action if he suspects I'm tired or may trip or, as in this case, catch a very excited Josh.

I give Lev a look as I wash vanilla icing off my finger. "I'm fine," I mouth.

He ignores me, leaning in with Josh in so he can give me a hug and a sticky kiss on my cheek.

"Sorry, Mommy."

"You don't have to be sorry, Josh. I love your hugs. Now tell me what you did," I ask as Gleb—it's still weird to think of him as my father, and I can't seem to be able to call him anything but Gleb—walks into the house looking a little tired after most of the day out with Josh.

"Grandpa took me racing! He's a really good driver, Mommy," he says that part with a nod in Grandpa's direction. Funny how he's taken all of this in. His new family, his new life. Not that this is his new life, but for a little boy who just one year ago thought he didn't have a dad and was too young to ask why, he now has a dad and a grandpa, and he acts like it's the most normal thing. Like they've always been there.

"Racing?"

"Formula 1, Mommy!"

"Where did you do that?" I ask Gleb as he sits down at the table and starts to check his phone.

"Oh, there's a place near here I rented out." He waves the question away.

"He beat Uncle Maxim and even Dima. Beat them bad."

Uncle Maxim walks stiffly into the house, and

Dima follows. He's the only one who doesn't look worn out.

Lev grins at Maxim. "You really are getting old, man," he tells him.

"Lev." I jab an elbow into him and turn to Gleb. "You rented a whole place out?"

He looks up at me like what I'm asking is ridiculous. "Of course."

"We talked about this. He needs to be treated like a normal kid and have a normal life."

With a shrug of his shoulder, he makes a dismissive sound and eyes the cake warily. The icing is vanilla, but the neon blue food coloring makes it look not very natural. On top are sprinkled miniature marshmallows in more colors you'd never find in nature.

Josh has climbed up on a stool at the counter and is looking dreamily into his cake.

"Shouldn't you sit down? Rest?" Gleb asks me.

"I've been resting for months. I'm tired of resting. Hey, but I'm serious," I tell him, going to him and placing a hand on his shoulder. "Normal, okay?"

"Okay," he says, closing his hand over mine. "But he's my grandson. I can spoil him on his birthday."

"Fine."

We haven't talked much privately since everything, and I want to spend some time with him. Hear about my mother from him.

I'm grateful that my brain seems to have blocked out the actual events of the afternoon that led to my medically-induced coma. I hope I never remember what happened to me that day because the sliver of memory I do have—the blurry vision of Vasily as he told me to look at him, to make sure I see him as he killed our baby, a baby I wasn't even sure was there yet—still has me waking up at night covered in a cold sweat.

I don't understand that kind of evil, and I never want to.

Gleb smiles up at me. I see the sadness in his eyes, that regret or loss. He hasn't opened up much about how he feels. I don't think it's natural for him to do that, but I get the feeling the regret is for what could have been.

If my mother had come to him, I think he would have forgiven her. Would I have grown up with a father then?

No. Even if I'd had a dad, I wouldn't have Lev or Josh, and I won't give them up for anything in the world.

"Take my grandson upstairs, Katerina. There are a few more presents for him in his room."

"More presents?" I ask.

"I'm allowed to spoil him on his birthday, remember?" His gaze falls on Lev. "Lev and I will have a talk."

I glance back and forth between the two of them, and I wonder if Lev knows what this is about.

"Go upstairs with your mom, Josh," Lev tells Josh, who has just licked a little icing off his finger.

He hops off the table, and I take his hand. "Don't think I didn't see that." I wink at him as Lev takes a seat at the kitchen table, and just beyond them, I see the two men outside.

Gleb's house is in a highly secure compound outside of the city, but I don't think I'll ever get used to all the guards. With Vasily and Andrei dead, do we have other enemies? In a way, I guess being Gleb Mikhailov's daughter makes me a target, and it makes Josh one too.

Josh hums a tune as we make our way upstairs to his bedroom. It's beside ours with a connecting door between and about three times the size of our little cabin in Colorado.

I have to tell him not to get used to this. We will leave soon, I think. But as much as I love Colorado, a part of me wants to stay here to be closer to my father now that I've found him. Give Josh the family I never had.

I know, though, that Lev wants out of this life. He doesn't like staying at the house, but it was the best option while I was in the hospital, and we didn't want to move Josh too much until we figured out what to do.

"Wow!" Josh's eyes go wide when he opens his bedroom door.

"Oh...my God."

He runs toward his bed, probably unsure where to start as boxes and boxes wrapped in brightly colored paper litter every available surface on the bed and floor.

I walk into the room to sit down at the head of the bed, hating that I feel a little tired, and watch him as he begins to tear into the packages. I can't help the smile on my face to see him so happy.

Does he remember that day at the house with Andrei? Or those men at the rest area when we'd run? Will those events ever come back to haunt him later?

I touch the scar on my arm and remember the events that traumatized me. That made me who I am.

I can't take those terrible things away from Josh, but I can be there for him when he does remember.

Glancing at the nightstand, I pick up one of the photos. It's the one of my mom with Gleb, and they both look so happy. I have one exactly like this in my room too. And I think about my dream at the hospital.

"Don't worry, I'll take care of her," she'd said. Her. Our little baby girl.

"Mommy." Josh climbs up into my lap, and I

wrap an arm around him as he rests his head, then touches my mother's face in the photo. "Mommy."

"Grandma." I'm not sure he believes me.

"Grandma," he repeats and looks up at me with Lev's eyes.

He touches a scar under the freshly cut bangs I got to hide this newer one. His face grows darker when he does it, but he never asks about that time I was in the hospital. I guess he will later, when he's older. Instead, he shifts his little hand to my hair and takes a lock of it into his hand.

"I like your hair better like this. I like red."

"Me too, sweetheart. Me too." I kiss him on the top of his head and hold him for a long time. I think he's going to fall asleep, and just when I think I might, too, he stirs.

"Time for cake?" he asks.

26

LEV

"I know you're a proud man." Gleb studies me from across the table. "I know you'd do what it takes to make sure your family is comfortable."

"Always." A dark cloud lingers above me as I consider everything that's happened over the past year.

"I'm sure I don't have to tell you that I'm a proud man too." Gleb smiles, and we both chuckle. "I haven't had anyone in my life for a long time. But for the first time, I have a family in Kat, Josh, and you. And I like to take care of my family too. I've been doing a lot of thinking about how we can make this work."

"I'm open to suggestions," I say, "as long as we're both on the same page."

Gleb nods. "I've already spoken to Maxim. He wants to stay in New York. He's going to do some work for me at the club. Nothing too strenuous, but I thought it would be something to keep him busy."

"If he's happy with that, then I am too."

"Good." Gleb reaches into his pocket and retrieves something, but I can't see what it is. "As for Kat, well she hasn't said one way or the other what she wants to do."

"We haven't really gotten to that part yet," I admit. "We've just been trying to make sure she makes a full recovery before we commit to anything."

"I have an option." Gleb slides whatever's in his palm across the table, and when he lets go, it becomes apparent it's a set of keys. "I don't want a thank you. I don't want anything. I just want you to accept this without being too proud to tell me you can take care of your family on your own, or whatever you're about to say. I'm an old man, and I have everything I need already. So, if I can do this for my daughter, it would give me peace of mind."

"What is it?" I pluck the key ring from the table to examine it.

"It's a house in upstate New York," he explains. "And when I say house, I mean it's a fucking fortress. There's a lot of acreage, and it's very secure. A good place for Josh to grow up. Your name won't ever be on any of the papers. Neither will Kat's. As far as anyone is concerned, it belongs to a shell corporation that isn't associated with any of us. It's the safest place you're ever going to get, and I just want you to tell me you'll take it."

I look into the old man's eyes, and despite the brash quality of his voice, I can see how much this means to him. And I know he's right. There probably isn't anywhere else in the world that would ever be as safe as something he chose. He's a man who worked his way to the top of the Russian syndicate and managed to stay alive all these years because he's smart and careful.

"There's one other thing," he adds. "Something else to consider. This won't hurt my feelings either way if you say yes or no. But there's a guy up that way who has some contacts with local businesses. If you're looking to go legit, he can likely get you on one of the crews. But I have my doubts that a man such as yourself is going to want to take orders from some pimply-faced manager who has a god complex."

"Yeah." A smile curves my lips. "I don't think that's going to happen, but I have a plan and some seed money. I'm going to see what I can do with it."

Gleb folds his hands and dips his head. "Alright. So, what do you think about the house then?"

I fiddle with the keys in my hand and shrug. "I'm

open to it. But I have to talk to Kat first. Maybe take them up there to see it."

"I suspected as much," he says. "We can all go up tomorrow. Tonight, I'm going to have a few drinks and relax. That kid of yours is hard to keep up with."

"Holy crap," Kat whispers to herself as we get out of the car and stare up at the house that Gleb described as cozy on our drive up to Cooperstown.

Gleb is watching his daughter carefully, and he's trying not to let her see his nerves. But he wants her to like it. He wants both of us to like it.

"Lev mentioned you like log cabins," Gleb says.

Kat blinks at me. "Yeah, but this place could eat my log cabin for breakfast."

"It looks big, but it's only forty-three-hundred square feet. An ample size for a family with plenty of room for additions."

Kat's expression dims, and I squeeze her hand in mine. It's something that we haven't talked about extensively, but the tragedy still lingers in the back of all our minds. I know Gleb wants Kat to be happy, to put it behind her and consider having more grandbabies. This is his way of showing that, even if he doesn't put it as delicately as most would.

"I like the porch." I redirect the conversation.

The cabin nestled onto the hillside has incredible views of Otsego Lake, and it isn't hard for me to imagine my family sitting on the wraparound deck every summer, soaking it in.

"It is a beautiful porch," Kat agrees. "The view is incredible."

"Come on." Gleb gestures for us to follow and leads us toward the house. "It's even better inside."

The air smells different up here. Cleaner. Crisper. Much like Colorado. And it's only a few hours away from Gleb's house, so it would be easy enough for him to visit as often as he likes.

Using the keys on the ring Gleb gave me, I unlock the door, and we step inside, taking in the details of the space. The main room is a lofty, open floorplan with massive windows and the views that Gleb promised."

I tuck Kat against my side, wrapping my arm around her waist as Josh squeaks his shoes across the wood floor.

"This place is huge!" he belts out. "Can we go swimming?"

Kat laughs and shakes her head. "Not today. We didn't bring anything to swim in. But maybe another time."

Hope shines in Gleb's eyes as he points out all the features of the house. Somewhere between the stone fireplace and the master suite, I can see acceptance in Kat's eyes. But she's still hesitant. Inside, she's that same little girl who came from nothing. She doesn't know if she deserves all of this, and even though Gleb was the one to give it to her, I want her to know more than anything that she does.

"Let's go check out the outbuildings," I tell her. "Leave Grandpa Gleb here with Josh."

Gleb nods, and I take Kat's hand, leading her to the large shop on the property. Already, I can see a use for it. It isn't difficult to imagine myself in here, getting back to my roots and recreating the pastime that I loved. Spending hours in the shop with my father, I would take pieces of metal and turn them into something else. But right now, I have a different idea in mind as I shut the door behind us and flip on the lights.

"What are we doing?" Kat whispers.

"This." I hoist her up onto the workbench and wedge my body between her legs, dragging her face to mine.

Kat moans against my lips, and I take my time, tasting her. Touching her. Appreciating every second of the privacy that we rarely get these days. I've missed this more than anything, but I haven't wanted to push her either. My cock is a pulsing beast in my jeans, and when I finally pull away, Kat and I are both breathless, hungry, and needy.

"Why did you stop?" she murmurs, trying to drag me back to her.

"We can't." I rest my forehead against hers.

"Lev." She sighs out in frustration. "You've been treating me with kid gloves ever since I came home."

"Because I don't want to rush anything." I brush her hair back out of her eyes and kiss the new scar on her forehead. The constant reminder that I almost lost her.

"I think it's time," she whispers against my lips. "Time to put the past behind us and move forward. But I'm scared."

"I know you are, sweetheart." I stroke her hair and cradle her against my chest, a silent promise that I'll always protect her. That I'll never let anyone else take her from me again.

"Do you like this place?" I ask.

"I do." Her fingers tangle together in her lap. "But do you think it's too much?"

"No." My lips graze along the length of her throat, and she curls her fingers into my hair. "I think if you like it, then this is where we will raise our family. But if you don't, that's okay too. I just don't want you to make a decision based on what you think you should have. Because you deserve the whole fucking world, baby. And Gleb and I both want you to have that."

Her body trembles in my grasp, and I don't have

to look at her eyes to know she's fighting back her emotions. There have been a lot of emotional moments since I brought her home from the hospital. Every day is a battle to remember what we've already conquered, instead of the things we've lost.

"Daddy!" The door bursts open, and Josh comes bolting in with a breathless Gleb behind him. He offers us an apologetic shrug as we part, and I help Kat down from the workbench.

"What is it, little fella?" I lean down and muss up his hair.

"I like this house," he says decidedly. "Grandpa Gleb said I could have a race car bed if I want to."

"Oh, he did now?" Kat eyes her father with humorous disbelief.

"Yep." Josh nods. "And we can go swimming in the lake in the summer. And we can get a dog too."

"Sounds like you've got everything planned out." I suck in a breath and look at Kat. So does Gleb, and then finally, Josh.

It isn't long before she caves with the three of us looking at her. Her shoulders shake, and it's the first tiny laugh she's allowed herself to have since the news of our loss. It might not be a big deal to anyone else, but for a woman who's felt like she needed to punish herself for something she couldn't control, it's a huge fucking deal to me. For the first time in months, I feel like I can breathe again as I see that tiny spark of life returning to her eyes. And I'm starting to wonder if it really is the air up here that changes everything.

"I think it's settled." Kat looks at her father, her eyes shining with appreciation. "We're moving to Cooperstown."

27

LEV

"I don't understand." Kat glares at me, her fingers digging into my jacket. "Where could you possibly have to go without us?"

"One day, sweetheart." My lips graze her forehead, and she shudders beneath my touch. "That's all I'm asking."

"One day for what?" she croaks. "I don't want you to go anywhere. I need answers, Lev. You promised me. You said you were done with this life. Don't leave."

"Kat," Gleb interrupts, saving me from having this conversation right now. "Lev has to go. He won't be gone long. In the meantime, you can help me pick out some furniture for the house."

Kat looks set to argue, but I give her a quick kiss

just as Josh comes flying into our path, tugging at Kat's leg. "Can we go swimming now?"

"Take the boy swimming." I squeeze her hand in mine. "And don't be too pissed off at me. I'll be back just as soon as I can."

Kat calls after me, but Gleb steps in and gives me a moment to make a quick exit. It's not that I want to leave her behind, but there's just one more thing I need to do. One final piece of the past to chip away so Kat can truly live in peace. An unfinished promise, and one last act of violence that I will gladly allow to stain my soul.

PHILLY IS DARK AND DREARY, and gray clouds blanket the sky with a silent threat to open up and unleash at any moment. Kat has already called and texted me too many times to count, and a part of me feels like an asshole for ignoring her right now. But I'm hoping that when she sees me again in the early hours of the morning, she'll come to understand.

The first stop I make is at my old house, which, by all appearances, has been left untouched. Not surprising, considering I paid everything for a year at a time. But I know when I open the door, it won't be the same inside, and it isn't. Judging by the shattered lamps and slashed furniture, it looks like Vasily and his men turned this place upside down. I can only imagine how frustrating it must have been for him not to find anything. He would have liked for me to be so stupid. But there are only two things that hold any sentimental value for me in this house. The rest means nothing.

I make my way into my bedroom and pull the area rug back. I guess Vasily never thought to look here, but even if he had, I doubt he would care about the old black garbage bags stashed in my hole beneath the floorboards. There isn't anything condemning about them, except for the fact that I'd kept them all these years, often sorting through them, hoping to get one last hint of her scent as it started to disappear. I don't know that Kat will actually want any of the things in these bags, but it's always been my goal to return them to her, just in case. It's one of the only promises I've ever been able to keep, and I want her to have her belongings from the old apartment, even if it just means she decides to dispose of them herself.

Next, I make my way into the garage. The few boxes I had stored here have all been torn open and scattered about, but the contents of the old metal storage cabinet are still in there, on display with the doors wide open. To Vasily, they would have meant nothing. But to me, these are the link to my past. One of the only good memories I have. Things that my father and I made together, and hopefully, something I'll be able to teach Josh someday too.

I look over the pieces, bits of rusty car parts welded into clocks, mirrors, animals, robots, or whatever my father was into at the time. Even after all these years, I think they still look pretty cool, and I'm banking on the fact that the public will too. My father had a dream of quitting his job at the steel factory and doing this full-time. That was before the days of online everything, but now it's more feasible, and I think I'm going to take a solid crack at it. Right now, I just can't imagine myself doing anything else.

After I've loaded up my car, I take one last look at the little house I used to call home. But it was never really home, and I realize that when I think about what's waiting for me back in New York. But before I get back to my real home, I just have one last stop to make. I plug the address into my GPS, and twenty minutes later, I'm driving through one of the most decrepit neighborhoods in Philly.

As I consider that, I think maybe I'm not even the worst thing that will ever darken the doorstep of the woman I'm looking for. Maybe the fact that she lost everything and had to move here in the first place was a fitting twist of fate. But I don't believe in karma. I never have. A man like me doesn't leave anything up to fate. I make my own revenge, and I don't regret it.

My GPS chimes, alerting me that the house is just up the block on the right. This doesn't look like the type of area where anybody would call the cops to help their neighbor, but just in case, I park my car next to an abandoned grocery store. Studying the shadows on the street, I listen for any signs of life. It's after midnight, and the only thing I can hear is the sound of a distant siren and a couple of alley cats establishing their territory as they skitter past me.

I move quietly, counting the houses and checking the mailboxes before I find the small, one-bedroom hole with a shoddy chain-link fence around it. There's no security. Not even a dog. It makes my job easier, and when I slip around back, there isn't even a goddamn deadbolt on the door. This woman is either very stupid or very naïve.

It takes me all of a minute to jimmy the lock. And once I'm inside, the smell of decay burns my nostrils. The house is full of trash with dishes rotting in the sink and cigarette trays overflowing with ashes. It's enough to make me want to puke, and I can't even imagine Kat ever living in conditions like this. I can only hope that this happened after she lost her husband and her entire life imploded, which would be the only logical conclusion, given Kat's previous descriptions of her. It's only fitting that her entire life has gone to shit, and I hope she regrets every second of every day that she pretends to be a woman of faith. But either way, she's about to atone for her every sin.

When I step into the hallway, the floorboard creaks, and at the same time, the bathroom door swings open. The shadowed figure in her nightgown opens her mouth to scream as she registers me standing there, the devil at her door. I slap my hand over her mouth, slamming her against the wall, and shining my flashlight into her eyes as I study her face for confirmation.

She looks fucking terrified, but almost resigned, like she somehow knew this day would come. A reckoning, the likes of which she's never seen. A snarl curls my lips, and I move the light away, allowing her to glimpse the monster before her as I drag the picture of Kat from my pocket.

"Hello, Mrs. George." I hold the photo up in front of her face. "You don't know me, but I know you. And this woman? She's very important to me, so I think it's about time we have a little chat about her."

28

KAT

I'm sick with worry for the next day and a half. Gleb knows where Lev is. At least he knows something. I'm learning Gleb's tells. The way his eyes shift just a little to the left of you when he's omitting something, even if he's not outright lying.

The times I've asked him directly, he's told me it's not a woman's place to know "these dealings" in this man's world, which is bullshit.

I vacillate between anger and paralyzing fear. Anger at Gleb and Lev for their secrecy, fear that he's gone to do another job. But what if there's one more after this one and another after that? I can't live this life. I can't let Josh live it.

Frustration and worry have me in the kitchen at four in the morning, pouring myself a glass of vodka. I stand at the glass doors and look out into the vast back garden, the trees of the forest behind which is a twelve-foot solid wall topped with barbed wire.

This place is a fortress.

Our house will be a fortress.

But if taking it means we're a part of this life, if taking it is somehow me giving my blessing for Lev to continue the work he's been doing, then I can't. I'll walk away. I'll have to no matter the cost.

I wonder if either man would let me, though.

A sound from inside the house has me turn toward the living room through which I can see the foyer. I hear the front door open. Two men speak in hushed tones in Russian, and I find myself exhaling. Thanking God.

The door closes. Quiet footsteps head to the stairs.

I set my glass down on the counter and hearing it, he turns, and when I see his face even in the dimly lit rooms, I think how much I missed him. How much I still miss him.

He hasn't touched me since everything happened. I know he's scared to hurt me, but I need him. Doesn't he know that?

After watching me for a small eternity, Lev walks through the living room and into the kitchen. He looks at me but doesn't speak. He eyes my drink, picks it up, and swallows the rest of it.

"What did you do?" I ask.

He takes the bottle and pours a second glass. He looks like he hasn't slept. Like he should be drinking a cup of coffee and not the vodka he's polishing off.

I put my hand over his when he pours one more glass.

"What did you do, Lev?"

"I buried the past," he says and swallows that glass too. When he sets it back down, he's finished with the vodka and moves around the counter toward me.

I turn with him, my back to the counter when he puts his hands on either side of me, his body against mine.

He needs me, too. I can feel the urgency of that need.

Leaning his head down, he kisses me. It's tentative at first, but when I wrap my hands around his shoulders, around the familiar, comforting strength of them, he cups the back of my head, and that kiss turns hungry. Ravenous.

He lifts me up, still kissing me as I wrap my legs around him. Carrying me to the kitchen table, he shoves the chair loudly out of his way and sets me on top of the table, breaking our kiss for the briefest moment to rip the silky nightie I'm wearing to the waist, exposing my breasts.

He groans, eyeing them, then dips his head down and closes his hungry mouth over one, sucking it into his mouth, dragging my nipple out with his teeth as I arch my back and push myself against the hard length of his cock.

I need him. I need him inside me.

"Lev." I reach for the buckle of his belt and open it.

He shoves my hands away as he pushes me backward to give equal attention to my other breast. His teeth are harder on my nipple than they were a moment ago, and it feels good.

I need to come.

I need him inside me, and I need to come.

"Kat." He moans against my mouth when he kisses me again. Pushing my nightie up, he rips my panties in his haste to get rid of them.

Then he bends his head to taste me.

"Fuck. I missed this. I missed this so fucking much."

I pant, wanting his mouth on me, wanting him to suck my clit hard and make me come, but I want him inside me more. I slide my hand into the waistband of his jeans and tug him closer, feeling the rock-hard muscles of his abdomen as I do.

He kisses me, pushing my clumsy hands away, then undoes his jeans, and shoves them and his briefs down.

"I don't want to hurt you," he starts, and I watch

him fist his cock. He wants this. I see it. Feel it. He's as desperate for this as I am.

"I need you to. I need you to fuck me hard, Lev. I need to know I'm yours again."

He stops, looks at me like he's confused, then cups the back of my head with one hand and brings my mouth to his, kissing me as he guides his cock to my entrance.

"When did you think you weren't mine?" he asks, pushing into me, tentative at first, like the kiss, but I can feel the frenzy just behind that caution.

"Whatever gave you the impression you weren't mine?" He thrusts hard.

I gasp when his body is flush against mine, his cock buried deep inside me. It hurts. It's been so long, too long, but this is exactly what I need.

"Show me," I tell him. "Show me I'm yours."

"Fuck, Kat." He groans against my mouth, moving inside me, fucking me, but I know he's still holding back.

"Hard, Lev. I need it. I need you to be like you were. No more kid gloves."

He stops, then cups my face. His hair sticks to his forehead, and his eyes burn black. His fingers are rough against my cheeks. He nods once, and one hand slides to the back of my head, and when he tugs my hair, I make a sound, a grunt as he forces my head backward and kisses my throat, then shifts one hand to my shoulder, bracing me as he drives into me with urgent, short breaths, his burning eyes never leaving mine.

When I come, I come hard.

He pulls my hair, and I cry out. He thrusts one final time with an animal sound, and when he stills, I feel him pulsate inside me, and we watch each other like this. Here but not here. Together as we pant and come, and when it's over, I'm spent. Limp. We both are as we lie against the table, catching our breath, sweat dripping from his forehead onto my cheek.

"Never doubt that you're mine," he croaks like they're all the words he can manage. "You will always be mine."

When I wake the next morning, it's to find Lev leaning up on one elbow smiling down at me and pushing hair back from my face.

I'm groggy as I meet his smile with my own.

"How did we get upstairs?"

"You don't remember?" he asks, raising his eyebrows and sliding his fingertips over the length of my bare shoulder.

But then it comes back to me, and a blush burns

my cheeks as I recall *what* we did when we got upstairs.

"There you go." He sits up, and I do the same, tucking the blanket over myself.

"What time is it? Why hasn't Josh come barreling in here?"

"It's ten, and I think Gleb's keeping him busy."

I turn to Lev, my face serious again as I study him. No cuts or bruises. But I remember the question from last night that he never answered.

"What did you do, Lev? Where did you go? I need you to tell me."

He gets up out of bed and pulls on his jeans.

When he does that, I reach to grab his discarded T-shirt and slip it over my head, sitting up and watching as he picks up his leather jacket.

He used to have one like it before too. That and the white T-shirts he still wears. I remember how I pretty much fell into him the first time we met and smeared magenta lipstick across that pristine white shirt. It feels like an eternity ago. Another lifetime.

"I brought your things," he starts. "From the apartment you shared with Rachel."

"What?"

"I collected them the night you took off."

I remember Rachel telling me that.

"They're in my car."

He carries his jacket over and takes two things

out of a pocket, then sets the jacket aside and sits down.

"Do you remember what I promised you a long time ago?" he starts, still keeping what he's holding out of my sight but picking up my arm and turning it over to trace the scarred skin, compliments of Mrs. George after she made me burn the record of abuse Joshua and I had been keeping.

I feel my face drain of blood and my stomach tighten.

"What did you do, Lev?"

"I promised you I'd punish her. And I promise to punish anyone who ever tries to hurt you or our family again."

"Lev?"

"She doesn't deserve your tears. She paid. And she's gone now."

He opens his hand and lets what he's holding fall, my gut clenching as I recognize the chain that's unraveling. The hideous cross that dangles from it.

My hand is at my mouth, and I lean away, my eyes locked on that thing. That cross she'd clutch. I can almost hear her voice, hear her prayers while she stood by as he did what he did to us.

"Hey." Lev closes his hand around it, eyes urgent on mine when I lift mine to his. "I thought...fuck, I don't know what I thought. I'll get rid of it."

He turns to walk away, but I catch his arm.

"No. It's not...you didn't do anything wrong. I just...seeing it again..." I swallow back the lump in my throat and steel my spine. "Give it to me." I hold out my hand.

"I'll take care of it. Get rid of it."

I shake my head. "I need to do that. I need to bury it."

He studies me for a long time, then finally pockets the thing.

"Lev—"

"We'll do it together."

"But—"

"There's something else. Something much more important, Kat."

He shows me the other thing, and my heart hammers against my chest in anticipation of what other piece of the past I'll be confronted with.

"I know you lost your scarf. The one Joshua gave you. I know how important it was to you."

My face falls a little at the thought. After what happened with Vasily, the hotel had cleared out our room, but when Lev picked up what was there, the scarf wasn't among our things. I'm not surprised. It was so ragged they probably thought it was trash.

"It's okay, Lev. I—"

"I found this. It's not the same thing, but I thought you'd want to have it."

I'm afraid to look down as he turns it over and

holds it out to me, but I do, and this time, it's like something squeezes my heart. I reach out to take the wrinkled old photograph.

Joshua and me. Cassie took the picture with one of those instant cameras. The photo is faded, but I can still make it out.

"We can see about having it restored," he says.

I can't answer him. There's a lump in my throat I can't quite breathe around, and I wipe away a tear.

Joshua and me in Halloween costumes. We're both skeletons. All three of us were. The Georges wanted to show us around town, their charity cases.

"She had it framed beside her bed if you can believe that," Lev says.

In the photo, I'm smiling, leaning my head on Joshua's shoulder. He's taking a bite of a huge Snickers bar and laughing around it. In my hand, I have my jack-o'-lantern to carry our candy.

We'd had fun that night.

"Kat? You okay? Shit, another bad idea?"

I shake my head and look up at him, hugging him, letting myself cry for a moment when he can't see me. Letting myself mourn once more.

"It's in the past now. If I could bring him back, I would, but I can't, and the rest, it's done. She's dead. It's over. Bury it, Kat. Let's have a future."

He draws back, digs something out of his pocket. It's a small box. I recognize that special, happy blue.

I look up at him, and he's watching me. He takes both my hands in his and just touches his mother's ring, which I'm still wearing on my right ring finger.

"Time to make it official," he says.

"What did you do?" I ask, my tone different than the last time I asked the same question.

He opens the box and turns it to me, and I try to imagine Lev in a Tiffany store, and it makes me laugh. I don't know. Maybe I'm just nervous, but I can't help it.

"That's not exactly the reaction I expected."

I look up from the engagement ring. The platinum band holding a single, perfect diamond at the center. Simple and elegant and...

"I love it." I throw my arms around his shoulders and hug him hard. He hugs me back, dropping the box on the bed when he does, holding me so tight.

I wonder how I'd survived so long before he found us. How I survived when he wasn't there to hold me like this.

He draws back, and there's a warmth in the air, something just for us.

"Will you marry me, Katya?"

SIX MONTHS LATER

EPILOGUE 1
KAT

I look at my reflection as the hairdresser pins my veil to the chignon she'd made earlier. She has set my bangs off to the side and has curled a long strand to fall softly over my right temple.

The dress is beautiful. It's absolutely not something I would have chosen or even looked at simply because the price was insane, but Gleb insisted. I would have argued except that when I turned to look at him and saw the tears in his eyes, I couldn't.

But the veil. My goodness.

It's a cathedral length ivory veil of the most intricate lace I've ever seen. It was my grandmother's, apparently, and I love it. I love everything about it.

"Just one more thing," she says, turning my chair a little and picking up a tube of coral lip stain.

I sit patiently as she dabs the littlest bit on.

"Perfect," she says, and when I look at myself, I think yes, it's perfect. I'm ready to marry Lev now.

The thought gives me goose bumps.

"Thank you," I tell her as a knock comes on the door.

"My pleasure."

She begins to clean up her things as the door opens, and I see Gleb standing there wearing a very fancy suit. Beside him is Josh, wearing a matching one and holding a piece of paper in his hand. Dima stands behind them, out of the way but always close at hand.

"Wow," Josh exclaims, drawing the word out when he gets a look at me. He walks toward me slowly, eyes wide.

"You look handsome," I tell him, adjusting his collar when he's close enough.

"Mommy, you're beautiful." I remember how he used to say booful what seems like just weeks ago. Time is moving too fast.

"Don't make your mother cry," Gleb says, but when I look up at him, he's looking a little emotional too. "Give her the drawing, Josh, and then you'll need to get ready to go to the church. Your dad won't want to be late."

"Here, Mommy, it's for you."

"Thank you." I open it to see his drawing. Crap. I'm definitely going to cry and ruin the makeup.

"It's you and Daddy and me and Grandpa."

"I love it," I say. "It's perfect." I hug him to me.

"Dima," Gleb calls.

Dima is inside the room in an instant.

Gleb gestures for him to take Josh. It's funny to see Dima, a soldier, in this role with Josh. I'm not sure he likes it. I think he does, but babysitting wasn't what he was hired to do.

"See you at church, Mommy. Don't be late."

I have to smile. "See you at church. You make sure Daddy isn't late."

Once they're gone, Gleb sits down on the edge of the bed and reaches into his inside jacket pocket. From there, he retrieves a velvet box. He opens it and seems to disappear into his own memories for a long moment.

I watch him, this powerful man, this ruthless man. I've done some research, and I have no illusions about who he is, but with me, with us, he's different.

He looks up at me. "I would have forgiven her, you know."

My mother. I nod because I do know.

"I know better than anyone else not to punish a person for past mistakes. Vasily blackmailed her over something I already knew. My mistake was in not telling her."

I remember something then. Something Vasily said about what my mom had done. What she was.

"Did she think I was so smitten I wouldn't look into her past?" Gleb continues. "But that's innocence. And my Ciara was innocent."

"Vasily said she was an escort."

"Did he tell you she was in this country alone? In this world alone? Did he tell you it was safer than the street for her? Did he tell you what it was like to be hungry? No, I don't think he ever knew that. I've known hunger. And I know what you'll do when you're desperate. Your mother had no family left, Katerina. She came to America looking for a better life and got mixed up with us. I choose to remember who she really was, not the things she did to survive."

"How did she meet your sister?"

"At a nightclub. I never liked her going to those places, but my sister was as stubborn as me." He smiles with the memory. "At least she took soldiers with her. Ciara had some trouble with a man, and Katerina saw it. I think that's when my sister appreciated having those soldiers. She and your mother became good friends, and I met her through Katerina." He looks off for a moment. "I was charmed from the first moment I laid eyes on her." He smiles. "There was her beauty, of course, but it was so much more than that. She was kind. I saw it in her eyes just as I see it in yours. Which brings me to this."

He looks at the contents of the box, then turns it to me.

I gasp because inside is the most beautiful pair of sapphire earrings I have ever seen. In a silver antique setting, they're almost too beautiful to touch.

"They were hers. A gift from me. She left them behind when she ran away. I think she didn't want me to think she was taking anything that didn't belong to her. As if I would." He shakes his head. "They're yours now, Katerina. And you must wear them today. What is this American tradition? Something old, something new, something borrowed, something blue. This takes care of old and blue. The dress is new. Put them on."

"Are you sure? I don't want to take—"

"Put them on." I hear the voice of the Gleb I met that first night. Mob boss Gleb.

I take the earrings and slide each of them on, making sure the back is twisted on tightly. I look in the mirror, and they are perfect with my hair and eyes.

"They're beautiful. Thank you for giving me something of hers." I hug him.

He nods but is stiff, obviously surprised. I'm surprised by the hug, too.

"As for something borrowed..." He stands, starts to look around. "I didn't think—"

"It's covered," I say, pulling the sleeve of my dress up to show him the bracelet Josh had made for me while I was in the hospital. "Josh took it back and lent it to me for today, but he says I can have it tomorrow for keeps."

Gleb chuckles. "Smart boy, my grandson. Are you ready?"

I take one last look at myself and stand. "Thank you," I tell him. "Thank you for everything, Gleb." I stop, shake my head. "Dad."

I realize it feels right to call my father Dad now. Not Gleb.

"You make an old man happy, Katerina. You and Josh and even Lev." He hugs me then, a big, warm hug. The first real hug I've had from him. He's been so afraid to hurt me, thinking I'm too fragile after everything that we haven't even hugged.

"You make me happy, too, Dad."

EPILOGUE 2

LEV

I've never been so fucking nervous in my entire life. Standing at the end of the aisle in my penguin suit, tugging at the collar that feels as if it's going to suffocate me. Josh is right beside me, my best man. He's dressed up in his own black suit, hair combed to the side, fingers clutching the ring "safe" he was intent on using. It's actually a toy safe, but when we told him how important this job was, he took it to heart. Just like his father.

He gives me a smile that feels like it's meant to be reassuring before he returns his attention to the box, intent on protecting it. The beating pulse of my heart feels like it's echoing off the walls as I look out at the men in the pews. We all look a little uncomfortable being in a church, but I can't imagine doing this anywhere else. Kat deserves the best, even if that means a room full of Russian mobsters in a place of worship.

We don't have a lot of friends or family to call our own, but the ones we do have are all gathered here today. Maxim, Gleb, Alexei and his family, Pasha, Dima, and some other trusted Vory who are here as guards. They are probably all about as comfortable as I am right now, dressed up in their nicest clothes, wondering if they will spontaneously ignite in this holy building.

Maxim clears his throat, and I look up. He smiles and nods to the end of the aisle, and there she is. My angel with red hair in a beautiful white dress. Somewhere in the background, the music starts, but I can't hear a thing as my gaze collides with hers.

I'd be lying if I didn't admit that a part of me questioned if she'd actually show up. After all the shit we've been through together, I wouldn't blame her. But I wouldn't let her go either. Kat knows if she ever runs, I'll be there to chase her. But as she walks down the aisle with Gleb beside her, I don't think I have to worry about that anymore. The conviction on her face is as certain as the sun will rise in the morning. This is meant to be. She and I until the end of the world or our bodies turn to ash—whatever happens first.

When she reaches the end, and I extend my arm for her, I feel like I can finally fucking breathe again.

But Gleb isn't so quick to hand her off. Even though I know I already have his approval, I can still respect him for turning to me with a warning before he lets her go.

"Take care of my little girl, Lev."

"Always." I smile back at him like a fool in love.

Kat smiles too, and we look like a bunch of goofy characters from a Hallmark movie, but I don't give a fuck. She's mine, and I'm hers, and this is the best goddamn day of my life, so I'll smile if I want to.

Maxim stands in front of us, poised and ready as the officiant, and I don't know who's more serious about their role between him and Josh. To me, it's merely a formality when Maxim begins to recite the words that will link Kat and me together for life. In our hearts, minds, and souls, we are already bound for eternity. I've never been more certain of that as I repeat the vows that promise I will love her in sickness and in health, good times and bad, wealth and poverty. But in my head, there is so much more. I will love her until she's old and gray. Pissed off and moody, or a shining beacon of light. I will love her in the blackest of times, and the brightest of times. In that, there is no question. My devotion to her will not waver, and I make it a point to slip that in as a whispered promise, something only she can hear.

Her eyes are glassy when she nods, whispering, "Me too," under her breath.

When it comes time for the rings, Josh is a total professional, smoothly unlocking his safe and forking them over reluctantly. Kat and I both tell him what a good job he's done, while Maxim sneaks a wink in his direction, making him beam proudly.

We finish the ceremony with a few of the traditions Gleb asked for, which included us both being crowned and stomping a couple of crystal glasses to bits. It makes no difference to me, and Kat was happy to include some of her familial roots in the ceremony. We could have gotten married anywhere she wanted, and I would have indulged her request. As long as Kat is happy, I'm happy too.

Never more so than when I finally take her hands in mine, and Maxim announces us as husband and wife.

"You look pretty well satisfied," I murmur, draping my arm over Kat's shoulders and tucking her into my side.

We're both naked in our master suite, exhausted but content from the night of celebrations. The crickets are chirping outside the window, the lake gently lapping against the shore, and there's a sense of peace between us that I'm fairly certain neither of us has ever felt.

"Are you sure you don't want to go anywhere for the honeymoon?" I ask her again. "It's not too late."

"No." She sighs in contentment, leaning her face against my shoulder. "I've seen too many hotel rooms to count. And I'm happy to stay right here. I think this is all we need."

"If that's what my wife wants." I kiss her on the temple, and she grins.

"How do you think Gleb and Maxim are going to handle looking after Josh for the next few days?" she asks, a hint of worry in her voice.

"I think they'll survive just fine," I tell her. "They did a great job when you were in the hospital. But if you want him to come home to us, there's nothing stopping that from happening either."

She sighs in relief and squeezes me in her arms. "This is why I love you. I think I'd like that. I'm just ready for our family to be together."

"I love you too, sweetheart." I bury my face into her neck and inhale her.

"Oh!" She sits upright, dragging her warmth away from me. "I almost forgot. I have something else for you."

"What is it?" I ask, but it's already too late. She's already bolting out of the room, giving me a nice view of her ass.

When she returns, she's wrapped up in a blanket, much to my disappointment, and she has a cupcake in her hand.

"You didn't get enough cake at the wedding?" I smirk, recalling how we smeared it in each other's face before sharing a sugary kiss.

"This one is different," she answers nervously, coming to sit beside me on the bed. "This one is for both of us."

I'm not sure what she means by that, but when she sets it into my palm, she explains.

"I had a bakery make it special just for us. There's a surprise inside, so we both have to pull it apart at the same time."

"Okay." I study her face, still uncertain why she looks so nervous. But it's making me anxious too, and now I want to open this fucking cupcake to see what's going on.

Kat and I both grip a side, and she counts to three. We tear it in two, and a tiny piece of paper wrapped up in plastic falls out.

"What the...?"

"Open it," she insists.

I unfold the plastic and unravel the scroll to reveal a photo. A sonogram photo.

I blink up at her, and her eyes shine with tears. It takes me a few seconds to catch up, but once I'm there, I'm choking on my own words.

"Are you telling me you're—"

"Pregnant." She finishes for me with a nod.

I drag her into my lap like a caveman, tossing the cupcake aside and clutching her face. "Are you sure?"

"Yes, Lev." She laughs. "Didn't you notice me getting fat?"

"You aren't fat." I frown. "You're as beautiful as always."

"Well, this little belly isn't from stress eating," she assures me. "We're having a baby."

A million different thoughts war in my mind. I want to be excited, but I can't lie because I'm fucking terrified too. Kat must recognize that in my face, and she touches me with a gentleness only she can possess.

"It's okay," she whispers. "We're past the three-month mark. We're safe, Lev. Everything is going to be okay this time."

My forehead dips into hers, and our lips collide with a breathless, frantic energy. I'm going to be a dad again. We're going to have a baby. And this time, I get to be a part of all of it.

"I want to know everything," I murmur as I tear the blanket off her body and palm her belly. "I want to be there for every appointment this time. Every step. I'm going to take care of you. Tell me what you need."

Kat laughs, the sound like music to my ears. "I

don't need anything. Just this. Just you and me and Josh, and our baby. We can find out the sex soon if you want."

I pull her in for a slow, drugging kiss, and my cock stirs to life beneath her ass. Without thinking about it too much, I'm palming her tits and touching her body, silently worshipping this woman who I get to call mine, now and forever.

"I guess there is one more thing you can give me," Kat whispers into my ear as she grinds down on my erection. "How about another orgasm?"

"How about three?" I flip her onto her back and bury my cock inside her until we both collapse onto the bed in a heap, our hands tangling together in unity.

Without a doubt, this woman was always meant to be mine.

The End.

THANK YOU

Thank you for reading *MINE* and *HIS*. We hope you loved Lev and Kat's story and would consider leaving a review where you purchased the book.

Keep reading for a sample from A. Zavarelli's *Crow* and Natasha Knight's *Collateral: an Arranged Marriage Mafia Romance.*

SAMPLE FROM CROW
A. ZAVARELLI

Donovan's movements grow weak and sluggish as his blood supply is cut off and his air slowly slips away. I count the seconds in my head and block out everything else around me. Three... four... five... six...

Finally, when I think I can't possibly hold on another second, he goes limp against my body and Johnny comes over to check. He calls the match. I can barely even move as I crawl out beneath him, but the adrenaline drives me up as I scan the crowd around me. I find his crew and flash them an arrogant grin. *Take that you bastards.*

A few of them walk in to collect their fallen friend as the crowd filters out of the building. I wipe the blood off my lip and watch them curiously while I wait. I only need one of them to bite. One of them to take an interest in me. It can't be the Russians. They have multiple factions and way too many members to count. The only way to narrow down my pool of suspects is to go straight to the source. The club where it happened.

They're all tossing glances my way, but it's Lachlan that doesn't take his eyes off me. I can't tell if he's pissed off or impressed by the expression on his face. Naturally, he's going to be suspicious of me. They come to these fights every week, and he's never seen me here before. He's got no idea who I am, but I know a few things about him.

Word on the street is that he's twenty-nine years old. Born and raised in Belfast until he migrated to the states in his teens. Grandson of Carrick Crow, the underboss to Niall MacKenna. He runs Slainte and does God knows what else for the syndicate. The rest is a mystery I'm going to have to unravel myself.

My eyes rove over him, taking in every detail. He has a rounded jaw covered in what I'd guess to be about a week's worth of scruff. It's a mixture of coppery brown and just a couple shades lighter than the dark unruly hair that rests atop his head. His eyes are guarded and drawn together and probably the most fascinating feature about him. They harden what would otherwise be a soft and almost boyish face. There's something almost familiar about them, but I can't quite put my finger on it. Sadness, perhaps?

It doesn't seem possible, but it's hard to tell. At present, they are drifting over my body. It isn't a blatantly sexual glance, not at all. In fact, I can't get a read on his thoughts, which is unusual for me. This man is growing more mysterious by the second.

He stands like a fighter. I can tell by the way he carries himself, but I've never seen him fight here. His frame is jacked. Lean, strong, and solid. His hands are calloused in a way that can only come from boxing.

He clears his throat, and my eyes shoot up and lock onto his.

A dark energy crackles to life between us as I stare into those savage irises. They swirl with an intoxicating and vivid array of colors I can't drag myself away from. I'd swear they were gray, but the next moment they seem to change to blue and then back again. They are both stark and beautiful in a way I didn't expect. The windows to his otherwise cold exterior.

Violence. Lust. Confliction. Pain.

I draw in a breath and try to convince myself that the bombastic beat of my heart is from the fight alone. The thrill of knowing how close I am to getting my in. I think.

He still hasn't spoken. But he will. And when he

opens his mouth, I have no doubt he'll still have an accent.

I don't encourage him. Instead, I unbraid my hair and run shaky fingers through it. This little war of wills is unexpected. I bet a man like him is accustomed to women falling all over him. There are a few, waiting in the wings, hoping that he'll notice them. But they haven't dared to approach him. I guess I'm not the only one who's heard about his reputation.

As I'm considering it, I catch a glimpse of Donovan charging at me from the corner of my eye. He snarls as he lunges towards me, a need for destruction in his blood.

I dodge back and prepare to hold my ground, but it isn't even necessary. Lachlan swoops into action and slams his body into Donovan's side, spinning him around and yanking his arm into a locked position behind his back. It only confirms my earlier suspicion about him being a fighter. Judging by his speed and agility, he's a natural.

He leans in close and whispers something into Donovan's ear. Donovan doesn't take his murderous eyes off me, but whatever Lachlan said has snapped him back to reality. He reluctantly backs down and mutters something under his breath before walking away. It seems like it's over, but in the back of my mind, I worry that I may have to contend with him later. He doesn't look like the type who takes being defeated by a woman too easily.

After a conversation with his men that takes place out of earshot, Lachlan stalks over to me, the same dark expression on his face. It pains me to admit it, but he is handsome. He's also more reserved than I expected. A calm façade to accompany his quiet broodiness. It's a complete contradiction to the killer I know he is.

He pauses at the concrete pillar across from me, maintaining his distance and keeping his expression neutral.

"Sorry about Donny," he says. "He can be a bit of a tool."

Just as I predicted, there's still an accent. I totally underestimated the charm factor there. It's rare that I find myself tripping over words, but that's exactly what I'm doing right now. Still, I school my features and try to look unflappable. I need to focus on the Russian, I remind myself.

"No biggie."

"Is it not generally an unwritten rule for women to fight in these things?" he asks.

"Well..." I flash him a cocky grin. "Lucky for me I don't play by the rules."

I expect him to throw me a bone. A smile. A twitch. Something. But I get nothing.

"Ye defeated one of my best fighters tonight."

I can't tell if he means it as a compliment or not, but I take it as one. "Thanks."

Lachlan remains steadfast in his indifference, and I don't really know how to shake him of it. I need to play my hand carefully here.

"I don't recall seeing you around here before, *butterfly*."

The way he emphasizes my fighting name sounds like a threat all in itself. I hate to admit it, but this guy is a little more intimidating than I want to give him credit for.

I blink up at him, formulating a plan. I'm going to play up the fragile little woman card in hopes it'll soften him towards me when I pop back up later. I doubt he has any heartstrings to pull, but it can't hurt to try.

"I only fight when I need the money."

Lachlan narrows his eyes, and I know he isn't buying it. He taps his fingers against his thigh, and for a brief moment, I almost wonder if he's nervous. But then I notice his eyes darting to some men across the room. I turn and my face sours on visual impact. The frigging Russians. They're eyeing me off, but one of them in particular is looking right at Lachlan.

I flash them a sweet smile and wave. I hate them. I hate them all.

When I turn back to Lachlan, he seems agitated, but it dissipates quickly.

"I have to head on," he says. "Catcha, butterfly."

My jaw clenches to keep my mouth from falling open. At the very least, I hoped he'd ask me for a drink. My phone number. Something. But his blatant rejection stings, more than I want to admit.

I knew I should have flirted with one of his soldiers, but he totally cock blocked the hell out of that plan.

"Yeah," I grumble. "See you around then."

<u>CROW: Boston Underworld #1 is available in all stores now!</u>

SAMPLE FROM COLLATERAL

NATASHA KNIGHT

Gabriela

I open both doors and walk inside, closing them behind me and leaning against them to catch my breath.

It takes me one moment to realize something is off.

The room is dark, the only light filtering from the party outside. The balcony doors are closed but I still hear the sound of five-hundred of my father's closest friends getting drunk on his dime. Well, my mother's dime, really.

But it's not that that's off. There's a smell that doesn't belong here.

A look around tells me I'm alone. But the bedroom door, it's open. I know I'd closed it when I'd left.

I walk toward it. I don't make a sound.

No one should be up here. The soldier wouldn't have let anyone up.

I push the door wider and step inside. The smell, it's stronger in here and it's making me nauseous.

The room is too dark for me to see and I'm about to flip the light switch when a figure moves. Standing with his back to the windows, the light creates a sort of halo around him and he has the advantage. I can't see his face, but he can see mine in that same light.

I swallow, try to speak. "You're not supposed to be here," I finally manage, sensing something dangerous. And I remember for all the friends my father has bought, the number of his enemies is double that.

"No, I'm not," the man says, his voice a deep, sure timbre that ices my spine.

He takes a step forward and I take one back, my hand closing over the doorknob behind me.

Danger.

It ripples off him.

"What's that smell?" I ask before I can stop myself.

"Morgue," he answers, his voice low and hard.

He walks toward me, no hesitance in his step, and before I can move, he's standing just a few inches from me.

The smell clings to him and it's making me sick. When I cringe back, he leans toward me and I open my mouth to scream just as something clicks.

For a moment, I think it's a gun.

But then the room is bathed in soft, golden light. He'd just reached to switch on the lamp on the table beside me.

I exhale but my relief is short-lived.

The man is taller than my father. He's more than a foot taller than me and I'm wearing four-inch heels.

His disheveled hair is dark, eyes hazel and I think he's drunk. He must be. Only a drunk man would enter Gabriel Marchese's daughter's bedroom.

Or one with a death wish.

"Who are you?" I ask.

He doesn't answer my question. "I came with a gift," he says instead.

He tucks his hand into his pocket and for a moment, I wonder if he's going to pull out a knife or a gun. If he's going to kill me after all. Because I know this man is not my father's friend. Not even a business associate. And for the first time in my life, I think about the protection I've always lived under.

The protection that often felt more stifling than anything else.

"It's your birthday, isn't it?" he asks, cocking his head to the side, setting one hand on the door above my head. He's leaning so close that I can feel the heat coming off his body.

I swallow.

"How did you get up here?" There are guards everywhere.

He lets what he's holding dangle and my gaze shifts to it, to the pendant hanging off a gold chain. It's too dark to make out the details.

"You shouldn't be up here. The party—"

"I'm not here for the party. I'm here for you, Gabriela."

My blood runs cold at his words.

My father, as much as I hate to admit it, scares me. But this man is terrifying.

His lips curve into something wicked. A grin. A sneer. I wonder if he can feel my fear. Maybe smell it coming off me. Men like this can, can't they?

"Turn around."

"Why?" I ask weakly.

"So I can give you your birthday present."

"I don't want—"

"I said turn around."

"Please just go," I manage.

"Turn. Around."

It's an order.

I swallow. Turn.

He moves his hand from above me once my back is to him, so when he lifts the chain over my head and brings it down to set the pendant against the swell of my breasts, I smell that smell again. On the sleeves of his suit. On the skin of his hands.

I look down at the pendant, but he pulls it higher so I can't see it. Instead, I notice the ring on his finger, a heavy, dark ring.

But then those fingers touch my skin and it's like touching a live wire. I gasp, listen to the hammering of my heart, wonder if he hears it. If he feels that shock of electricity.

I don't move as he pulls the chain tight, the pendant at my throat. He tugs and a new panic takes hold. I think he's going to strangle me with it.

I make a sound, a pathetic whimper. I should scream but it's like my throat has closed up.

"It's broken," he says. "That's rude, isn't it? To give you a broken gift?" His deep voice is low, his breath on my neck sending a strange sensation down my spine. "But that's how I got it, too."

I realize what he's doing. He's tying the chain. He must be.

I reach my hand to touch the pendant and when I do, something crusty flakes off.

A glance at my fingers shows a flake of dark red and I know it's blood. I know it.

My stomach heaves and I tighten my muscles, trying to quell the urge to vomit.

"There," he says. I smell whiskey on his breath now that he's closer and hear him inhale as the scruff of his jaw scratches my bare shoulder and I shudder.

Undeterred, he tilts my head to the side and presses his lips to the curve of my neck. To my pulse.

My breath catches and I can't move.

It's not a kiss, this.

This man isn't kissing me.

But his lips, they're warm. And that disgusting smell of chemicals and death, it's going to make me sick. He must feel my knees give out because he wraps one powerful, muscled arm around my middle, tightening his grip as he holds me against him.

He brings his mouth to my ear, breathes in a deep breath.

"I want you to give your father a message for me," he starts, pausing for so long that it feels like the air is heavier for the unspoken words. For those that are still to come. "Tell him I'll be back to take something precious too."

An eternity passes before he steps backward.

My knees buckle, and I catch the doorknob to

remain upright. It's suddenly freezing in my room and I'm shivering.

"You won't forget to give him my message, will you?"

I shake my head. It's all I can do.

He nods, eyes narrowing, a smile that's not a smile at all turning the corners of his mouth upward.

"Happy birthday, Gabriela," he says, and with that, he's gone.

Collateral: an Arranged Marriage Mafia Romance is available in all stores now!

ALSO BY NATASHA KNIGHT

Ties that Bind Duet

Mine

His

Collateral Damage Duet

Collateral: an Arranged Marriage Mafia Romance

Damage: an Arranged Marriage Mafia Romance

Dark Legacy Trilogy

Taken (Dark Legacy, Book 1)

Torn (Dark Legacy, Book 2)

Twisted (Dark Legacy, Book 3)

MacLeod Brothers

Devil's Bargain

Benedetti Mafia World

Salvatore: a Dark Mafia Romance

Dominic: a Dark Mafia Romance

Sergio: a Dark Mafia Romance

The Benedetti Brothers Box Set (Contains Salvatore, Dominic and Sergio)

Killian: a Dark Mafia Romance

Giovanni: a Dark Mafia Romance

The Amado Brothers

Dishonorable

Disgraced

Unhinged

Standalone Dark Romance

Descent

Deviant

Beautiful Liar

Retribution

Theirs To Take

Captive, Mine

Alpha

Given to the Savage

Taken by the Beast

Claimed by the Beast

Captive's Desire

Protective Custody

Amy's Strict Doctor

Taming Emma

Taming Megan

Taming Naia

Reclaiming Sophie

The Firefighter's Girl

Dangerous Defiance

Her Rogue Knight

Taught To Kneel

Tamed: the Roark Brothers Trilogy

ALSO BY A. ZAVARELLI

Boston Underworld Series

CROW: Boston Underworld #1

REAPER: Boston Underworld #2

GHOST: Boston Underworld #3

SAINT: Boston Underworld #4

THIEF: Boston Underworld #5

CONOR: Boston Underworld #6

Sin City Salvation Series

Confess

Convict

Bleeding Hearts Series

Echo: A Bleeding Hearts Novel Volume One

Stutter: A Bleeding Hearts Novel Volume Two

Twisted Ever After Series

BEAST: Twisted Ever After #1

Standalones

Tap Left

Hate Crush

For a complete list of books and audios, visit http://www.azavarelli.com/books

ABOUT A. ZAVARELLI

A. Zavarelli is a USA Today and Amazon bestselling author of dark and contemporary romance.

When she's not putting her characters through hell, she can usually be found watching bizarre and twisted documentaries in the name of research.

She currently lives in the Northwest with her lumberjack and an entire brood of fur babies.

Want to stay up to date on Ashleigh and Natasha's releases? Sign up for our newsletters here: https://landing.mailerlite.com/webforms/landing/x3s0k6

ABOUT NATASHA KNIGHT

USA Today bestselling author of contemporary romance, Natasha Knight specializes in dark, tortured heroes. Happily-Ever-Afters are guaranteed, but she likes to put her characters through hell to get them there. She's evil like that.

Want to stay up to date on Ashleigh and Natasha's releases? Sign up for our newsletters here: https://landing.mailerlite.com/webforms/landing/x3s0k6

Printed in Great Britain
by Amazon